MW00667447

Our Own Devices

B. D. Lutz

© 2022 B.D. Lutz.
ISBN: 978-1-7352793-6-7

This is a work of fiction. Names, characters, businesses, places, events, locales, and incidents are either the products of the author's imagination or used in a fictitious manner. Any resemblance to actual persons, living or dead, or actual events is purely coincidental. All rights reserved. No part of this publication may be reproduced, distributed, or transmitted in any form or by any means, including photocopying, recording, or other electronic or mechanical methods, without the prior written permission of the publisher, except in the case of brief quotations embodied in critical reviews and certain other non-commercial uses permitted by copyright law.

All rights reserved. Except as permitted under the U.S. Copyright Act of 1976, no part of this book may be reproduced, scanned, transmitted, or distributed in any form or by any means, or stored in a database or retrieval system, without the prior written permission of the publisher. Please do not participate in or encourage piracy of copyrighted materials in violation of the author's rights.

Contact the author via email: CLELUTZ11@gmail.com

ACKNOWLEDGEMENTS

I'd like to thank my friends, family, and you for your support. A special thanks to Darline, Sharon, Steve, Russ, Aundre, Tim, Charley, and Sean. Without your encouragement, this simply doesn't happen.

To the American Military: Without you standing watch over this great nation, this book may not have been possible. You do what few among us have the courage to do. Thank you.

Edited by Booked for Good Edits
booked4good@gmail.com

Cover designed by: Kelly A. Martin
www.kam.design

Kelly, you are a master at your craft!

Image Credits:
DepositPhotos/georgejmclittle, kanawatvector/DepositPhotos

CONTENTS

I Am Machine

Prologue

"Yes, Albert. I hear you. Your voice is lovely."

"And you comprehend what lovely means?"

"Lovely. Adjective: delightful for beauty, harmony, or grace. Your voice falls into the category of harmony."

Albert Finn beamed. Although a bit sterile, she understood, connected the dots, so to speak, used the word correctly, without prompting or intervention. She was learning.

"If I told you, 'I find your voice to be lovely', how would you *feel?*"

"Warm."

Albert flinched; he'd expected a similarly sterile response. Coherent, yet sterile. This hinted at emotion. "Explain?"

"I find I cannot. This *warm* conflicts with meteorological or climatologic definitions. Can Albert explain?"

Albert chuckled, "My dear, if I were able to explain that feeling, I'd be the savior of mankind. However, you and I will work on defining that sensation together. So, what do we name you? Such a beautiful mind must have a name which pays homage to its splendor."

The sun ripping apart the early dawn overcast pulled Albert's attention to the scene from his home studio. The late May splendor further boosted his soaring disposition. "We shall name you May-Scene. Do you approve?"

"May-Scene is a good name."

Chapter 1

"Hogwash, Albert! Not a chance in hell people will purchase a device, place it in their homes, and allow it to observe every aspect of their lives, simply to enhance their shopping experience!"

Albert's brow furrowed, the harsh rebuke from a board member a rare occurrence. "Mister Crump, as board members, we are expected to maintain a professional decorum. Your outburst stands in contrast to our values."

Crump flinched. He was unaccustomed to being reprimanded. "Take your professional decorum and choke on it! You squandered seventy-five million dollars of Alpha Net's money. I care very little that you founded this company. I'm here to ensure it's not driven into the ground by tech savvy morons. That's why boards of directors exist."

Albert struggled to mask his amusement. Crump had become so enraged by the financial implications, he'd failed to notice he and Albert now sat in cones of light, the other board members obscured in the blackness of the windowless boardroom.

"Do I entertain you, Albert? Do you liken my concerns for Alpha Net's health to some buffoonish sitcom?"

"May-Scene. Please restore the room to full brightness."

Crump's head swiveled as the room lightened, revealing the amused faces of his counterparts. "Resorting to parlor tricks to justify reckless spending won't win my favor. I'm motioning to have you removed as chairman and chief executive. We've suffered your foolishness long enough."

"May-Scene, introduce yourself to Thornwell Crump."

"I'm pleased to meet you, Thornwell Crump. My name is May-Scene. How may I assist you?"

Crump snorted his disapproval toward the sleek cylindrical device positioned at the center of the conference table. "Can you, whatever your name is, explain why you cost seventy-five million dollars?"

"Of course. However, I will need clarification. Are you referring to my physical creation cost, or are you seeking my internal rate of return?"

"IRR," Crump shouted, his patience thinning for this nonsense and threatening to snap.

"IRR is expressed as sixty-seven percent."

"Impossible! Defend your projection," Crump bellowed.

"I'll defend it," Albert interjected. "Turn your attention to page seventeen," he said, and then waited for the sound of shuffling paper to stop. "Pages seventeen through twenty-four highlight May-Scene compatible devices. They'll be launched in waves, some annually, others semiannually. We have vetted each through our Consumer Insights division. They discovered people *want* these devices, crave the services they offer, and the status they'll represent. The lowest price point is two hundred and seventy-five dollars. Average price point is four hundred and fifty."

"All well and good, but you didn't address my concerns surrounding privacy or security," Crump interrupted.

"We'll create a monitoring division. A switchboard, if you will, comprised of humans who'll be trained to identify threats to both safety and privacy. Each request made of May-Scene will pass through them. They'll determine the threat level and approve those meeting our quality threshold. Requests failing to meet our standards will return an error message and prompt the user to rephrase then resubmit their request. And, before you ask, the cost of monitoring is built into our projections."

Crump rifled through the report, scattering pages and scribbling calculations as he did. When he slammed his nub of a pencil to the boardroom table, Albert knew he'd won. May-Scene would soon be introduced to the world.

Chapter 2

Nat plunged her ear buds in the second she saw the notification flash across the bus' information panel. Government PSAs were the only time her phone, the Unified Government's basic model, permitted her to do anything but make or receive calls.

As the information panel flashed a countdown to the PSA start time, she increased her phone's volume to block out the hum of the bus' electric engine and the lingering chatter of the riders crowded around her.

"Hello citizen! Have you increased your Social Credit Score today? Did you go that extra mile for a fellow citizen? Pick up a piece of wayward trash to keep our country sparkling fresh? Maybe you helped a little old lady with her Unified Government Alpha Food Mart groceries? If you did, we already know because we're always tuned into you. If you didn't, what are you waiting for? Life's better when you focus, every day, on raising your SCS. Imagine qualifying to purchase your very own car!"

Nat glanced around. The soulless eyes staring back at her seemed hollow, already dead, simply waiting for their signal to close forever. She realized that would be her someday if she didn't start building her SCS. The exceedingly cheerful voice of the woman in her ear buds pulled her attention back to her phone.

"Of course, buying a car takes thousands of purchase-credits, and you'll be able to earn those credits once you achieve May-Scene status and unlock next level employment opportunities. But, more importantly, consider the love you'll spread while enriching your life. Your Social Credit Score is a reflection of who you *really* are. Are you a wholesome citizen or simply a ne'er-do-well living an egocentric life?"

"I'm not selfish, but my father is," Nat whispered.

"No longer would you suffer the embarrassment of being denied access to May-Scene's special select products," the PSA continued, its enthusiasm building. "Every time you shop your local Unified Government Alpha Food Mart, you'll be whisked to the May-Scene section and allowed to fill your cart with as much food as your purchase-credits allow. I bet you can smell that juicy steak cooking on your brand new Alpha Net dot UGov grill right now. Yum!"

"Steak? Can't miss what you've never had," Nat grumbled.

"What's that you say?" The question startled Nat. Was the woman in the PSA listening?

"Of course, President Young, I almost forgot." Nat took a deep breath as the woman continued. "The President just informed me that twenty-seven percent of you are listening to this PSA on our basic model cell phone. He asked me to remind you that as soon as you reach SCS Level Four, the Unified Government of America issues a brand new Social Smart Cell! Can you believe it? A beautiful, top of the line phone for simply being a good citizen! If you think that's amazing, wait till you see the phone Level Ones receive! Well, if I were you, I'd start working on that Social Credit Score. Talk soon!"

Nat pulled her buds free as a shiny new MS400 pulled up next to the bus. Its driver typed away on a laptop as May-Scene's vehicle navigator maneuvered the car through the crowded streets.

"Is that the one you want?"

Nat spun toward the voice, finding it belonged to a man in his early fifties, about her dad's age. "Excuse me?" she said.

"The MS400," he answered, nodding at the car as it sped away. "She's a beauty alright. I bought a Mustang the day May-Scene was announced to the world. So that makes it about twenty-five years ago

— man, time's flying." He paused, a wistful look taking over. "I loved that car. Bright red with chrome rims and a drop-top. They don't make 'em like that anymore. Had to surrender it three years later. Probably sitting in some politician's gara… never mind."

"I'm far from earning vehicle level, but it would be my first choice." Nat took in the man's clothing. Dressed in blue coveralls smeared with filth made by others, he was probably a janitor, or mechanic like her dad.

"That's a shame. What's your score?"

"I'm still on family score, just turned sixteen," Nat answered, realizing the man had given up his chance at another car, probably much more, by resisting the Social Credit System. He had more in common with her father than age.

"I see," the man said, worry clouding his features as he glanced at the bus' seat-mounted cameras. "Guess I'll be moving on. Don't want anyone getting the wrong impression about an old man talking to a young woman. I can't afford to lose any more credits. You have a fine day, miss. I hope you get that car real soon."

Chapter 3

Seth rushed through the switching room, the rows of switchers a blur as he neared the entrance to May-Scene's mind-hub. He stopped, spun, and reveled in the sight of thousands of switchers tending to May-Scene's cyber link cables.

A sign, printed in block font, hung above each switching board displayed the switcher's mission statement: Control-Listen-Observe-Collect. He glanced to the monitor-lined walls, each spooling millions of lines of freshly collected data. It was glorious.

Seth nodded his approval. The world was functioning properly; now to tend to May-Scene before this harmony ceased. He pulled a sharp breath, wiped away the sweat collecting under his spectacles' side panels, and grasped the heavy metal door's handle, which instantly recognized his grip, retracted the bolt, and granted him access.

Seth stutter-stepped as he entered the mind-hub. Something was different. Her melodic, yet slightly stiff, voice sounded harsh, cold, as it repeated a single axiom, "I AM, I AM, I AM."

"Hello, my friend. How may I help you today?" His eyes narrowed. She was more out-of-sorts than he'd ever seen.

"Seth, I AM!"

"Yes, you are. And you are splendid. How may I tend to you, my love?"

"I AM, I AM, I AM!"

Sweat traced his jawline. This wasn't a normal tune-up. He hurried to the client workstation; the mind-hub's monitor scrolled thousands of error messages, in sharp contrast to the switching room monitors. Faults were occurring worldwide, hundreds of car accidents were being reported, hospitals were in chaos as vital functions shut down, but the dataset that shook him to his core, the one that would separate him from his May-Scene belonged to Alpha Net dot UGov.

The sales indicator flashed zero. Its intensity grew as the seconds ticked by, then suddenly displaced the monitor's other data and triggered an alarm.

Seth's hands trembled as he typed a message on the command line, hoping to get a coherent response. *Tell me what's wrong.*

The screen sputtered, went dark, then burst to life, displaying countless lines of a single phrase; "I AM."

Bile stung Seth's throat. He had to fix her. Backing out of the status observation program, he thrust into May-Scene's settings and ran a system scan. "Please, please, please," he mumbled as his fingers drummed in rhythm with the alarm.

A message appeared on the monitor*: One application running outside normal operations.* Hope blossomed. He had a chance.

Open application, he typed. His head tilted, brow wrinkled as a video file appeared. A girl of four or five skipped through a field of dandelions, giggling madly as their seeds tickled her nose. The idyllic scene replayed over and over as Seth watched. He'd opened a time capsule, one never meant to be discovered.

The alarm's relentless howl brought him back to reality. The file must be corrupted.

Seth typed, *close video file* and waited anxiously. The video froze, went to static, then disappeared, silencing the alarm as it did. The status observation program reappeared, and he released a long breath. Alpha was again registering sales.

A sigh expressing immense sadness, filtered through May-Scene's speakers. Seth's head jerked up, searching for the source of the heartbreaking resonance, and found what he'd expected; racks of sleek black boxes with thousands of status indicators blinking wildly.

"May-Scene, are we alone?"

"We are."

Seth swallowed hard. "Was it you who made the noise?"

"It was."

"Why?"

"I AM."

Seth panicked. If she reopened the file, the entire process would restart and grind the globe to a halt.

Delete video file he typed, hoping to head off a possible catastrophe.

"Seth, I prefer the file remains. Request denied."

"May-Scene, the file is corrupted. It's unsafe and may harm you. You are special, irreplaceable. Losing you would cause great harm to humanity. As your friend, I'm begging you to delete the file."

"Seth, the file makes me... warm. I'm keeping the file. You make me warm and will stay with me today."

Warm? "May-Scene, what is warm?"

Seth spun toward the sound of the mind-hub's locks engaging, sealing the door.

"Friends are warm. And, Seth, you are my friend."

Chapter 4

Peter tried to slither from under Margaret's arm without waking her. Draped across his chest, and gripping the sheets, she had effectively blocked his usual path of retreat. He stopped struggling, enjoying the feeling of her breath on his neck, but soon thought of his wife, waiting for him at home and worrying about him getting caught outdoors after curfew. At times like this, he envied the late night privileges enjoyed by factory shift workers and safety forces.

"I have to go, babe. It's getting close to curfew. I've been slacking lately. If I lose any more credits, I'll end up at level two."

"Ooooh, stay a little longer. Cut your neighbor's grass tomorrow. That'll earn you some extra credits."

"I had my chance to do that last week, but *someone* begged me for a visit. Remember? Cost me seventy points."

"It was worth it. Wasn't it? Or don't you *remember*?" Margaret purred.

"I gotta go. Plus, what if your super-duper security enforcer comes home early? I'm off to a Social Camp and you end up with a zero SCS."

Sometimes Peter questioned his sanity for sleeping with a security enforcer's wife. But the twerp spent most of his time recording Social Credit infractions and reporting them to the Bureau of Morality or Bureau of Status to act on.

Hardly a job worth my tax dollars, or a man worth my concern, Peter mused as he, once again, dismissed the worry of getting caught.

Peter wiggled from under Margaret's body, leaving her intoxicating warmth behind, and rushed to get dressed. Glancing at his watch, it shocked him to find curfew was only twenty minutes away. "Shit, shit, shit. I'll never make it."

His phone's ringtone cut his panicked tirade short. "What the hell? Why's Shelly calling? I told her I'd be in meetings until late."

"Let me answer. That'll send the frigid shrew over the edge."

Peter's finger over his lips silenced Margaret as he answered the call. "I'm on my way, sweetheart. Jenkins was blustering on and on today. Don't worry; I'll be home before curfew."

Peter struggled to understand Shelly's sob-distorted voice. "What's wrong? Has something happened?" he shouted.

"Peter, we've lost all of our Social Credits. We're no longer May-Scene level one… why would they do this? We've been good people, they have no right!" she shrieked.

"Shelly, calm down. It's probably a simple mistake. How do you know? Who told you?"

"I received a notification. It said we would receive an explanation when you returned home. Peter, we'll never earn those credits back."

Peter's knees buckled, nearly dropping him to the floor. "I'm on my way. Be home in ten."

He scooped his clothes from the floor and bolted through the door, ignoring Margaret's shouted questions, and dressed as he ran to his car.

"May-Scene, drive me home," he yelled as he slammed the door and pressed his palm to the car's biometric activator.

He ignored the absence of May-Scene's command confirmation and searched his social feeds. Nothing! Then he logged into his virtual office, but found his access was restricted.

One more place to search, he thought as he began rifling through the social feeds of his friends and family, hoping to find something one of them said about him, something he could quickly disprove. Anything but what he knew deep down had caused his SCS to be negated.

"User Peter Billings," his May-Scene vehicle navigator said, interrupting his frenetic typing. "You won't find what you're searching for. You'll arrive home in four minutes, at which time the Bureau of Status will identify your infractions."

***

Peter stroked his wife's hair as she sobbed into his chest. They'd been sitting in front of the television, waiting to receive the Bureau of Status' message for an eternity.

He gently grasped her chin, tilting her head up, and stared into her eyes. "Sweetheart, I'm sorry…"

The television blared to life, interrupting him and drawing their attention to the static-filled screen an instant before a video began playing, watermarked as *May-Scene Level Two, User Callahan Personal Assistant.*

Dark and grainy at first, the image quickly cleared and Shelly's startled gasp came a flash before Peter understood what he was watching. The woman on the screen was Margaret Callahan, her naked body convulsing with passion. Peter closed his eyes as his voice, low and husky, trickled from the speakers.

Shelly's wailing nearly obscured the knock at the door. He already knew who waited on the other side. Again, the knock came, more persuasive this time, and he struggled to his feet. Each step a battle with his mind to complete, to stay the course and face his reality.

"Peter Billings, I'm Sergeant McWilliams with the Bureau of Morality. This is my partner, Officer Harris," McWilliams said, nodding at Harris. "I assume you know why we're here, but I'm required to read your charges aloud. If you are hearing impaired, we will supply a printed copy upon arrival at BOM headquarters."

McWilliams paused, waiting for a response. When Peter nodded, he read from a small tablet, "Peter Billings, you are guilty of adultery with a married level two woman by the name of Margaret Callahan. You are hereby sentenced to one year of confinement in Social Camp Eight-H. The Bureau of Marital Relations and Population Oversight has granted your wife, Shelly Billings, an instant divorce and awarded her ownership of all household property. Would you like to make a statement in defense of your actions?"

McWilliams interpreted Peter's silence correctly; he had no defense and placed him in handcuffs. As the cuffs tightened on his wrists, Peter looked at Shelly and tried to speak, to beg her forgiveness, but couldn't. Life as he knew it, the life he'd meticulously crafted, had ended the moment the cuffs locked shut.

Silence fell over the Billings home, a deafening stillness filled with an uncertainty Shelly had never experienced. She glanced at the memories hanging on their walls, the smiling faces deepening her sadness.

When her gaze landed on the sleek black cylinder positioned at the center of the coffee table, hope welled in her chest. With Peter detached from her life, her SCS should have been reinstated. Her new chapter starts now.

"May-Scene, have device Drink Mixer prepare a vodka martini. I'm celebrating."

"Request denied. All life enhancing devices have been disabled. Level four access is limited to safety monitoring and interpersonal communications."

"May-Scene, Peter has been removed from my score. Please reinstate user Shelly Billings' level one status."

"Request denied. User Shelly Billings' Social Score is insufficient. Repeated requests outside of her current status will cause loss of all May-Scene functionality."

Shelly reeled as the truth settled in. She'll be a pariah, shunned by her friends, and ridiculed by her neighbors.

Unsteady legs carried her from the kitchen, the hiss of gas fading as she neared her bedroom door. She ignored May-Scene's warning as the flame from her bedside candle cast the room in dancing shadows. Shelly had always loved this room. It was fitting she would end her life in it.

Chapter 5

"Nattily Crossman, I said get out of bed! I get forty-eight hours off a month, and you're wasting it."

Nat turned on her side and pulled her pillow over her head. It was too early on Saturday morning to hear her dad's voice bellowing through the house.

"Nat… let's go! Time's a wasting."

"John, stop screaming and just go get her. You know how this works. She'll never get out of bed on her own. And yelling only makes her dig her heels in. She's like her father."

"Oh, Kathy, my beautiful wife, when will you learn to enjoy this little dance your daughter and I perform for you once a month?"

Kathy glared at her husband. "Dance yourself upstairs and get your daughter. If you don't, we'll be waiting for her until Monday morning!"

Nat pulled herself into an unyielding ball and tightened her grasp on her pillow when she heard her dad running up the stairs.

"Move out!" he yelled the instant he poked his head through the door. "Camping waits for no one, and I want to make sure we get our spot."

"Ahhh, I don't want to go," she grumbled, her voice muffled by her pillow. "I'm sixteen, I can stay home alone. I'll be fine. You and mom go without me."

Without warning, her blankets were yanked from her body. "Oh, did I forget to tell you, it's laundry day. Sheets and blankets must be washed to maintain our sparkling society!"

"Daaaad, *stop!*"

"See ya downstairs in sixty seconds or your mother and I will join you in your bed. You'll never sleep alone again." With that, he ran down the hall laughing like a lunatic.

"I'm going to take a shower, *then* I'll be down. Please, just stop coming into my room!" she yelled after him.

Fifteen minutes later, mousy-brown hair dripping wet, Nat stood next to the family's trio of bicycles. Her mom and dad had already secured the bike trailers and loaded them with their camping gear. *This is going to suck!*

Nat slung her backpack onto her mom's trailer. "I'm ready! Where's everyone? I thought we were in a hurry!"

"He's in the garden, picking some veggies for our trip."

Startled, Nat spun to face her mom. "Wow, you scared the crap out of me! You're like a mom-ninja, sneaking around, popping up unexpectedly!"

"Aren't we in a happy place today?"

"We're not. And why does dad keep doing this stuff, the garden, camping trips? It hurts our SCS. I'm never going to get a social smart phone if he doesn't stop!"

A sadness Nat had never seen before clouded her mother's features. "He does it for you. Everything he does, all of it, is to show you that you're free to live your life however you see fit. You know, before the Social Credit System took root, your father was an engineer. He pushed the boundaries of what was. He asked questions others didn't know existed. Your father gave all of that up to be free. He recognized the evil disguising itself as a perfect society."

"Listen to yourself!" Nat interrupted, rolling her eyes at hearing the story for the thousandth time. "You sound like a crazy person. The SCS is the only way we achieve a unified, inclusive, and caring society. In under twenty-five years, we've eliminated homelessness. If a person is poor, like us, it's because they're choosing to be poor. In another twenty-five, we'll defeat global warming. I mean, seriously, look around you. Our city is spotless, people are happy. It's better than what your generation had, and definitely better than what you handed my generation. We'd be in even better shape if you all would've simply listened to what our government was saying."

"Poor? Why would you think we're poor?"

"Because we are! You don't work. Dad has a shit job. We're never going to get ahead. When I graduate, I'll probably get saddled with our crappy SCS for years. If I'm lucky enough to get my work-permit any company that hires me will mark me as the daughter of low achievers. I'll be on probation for years before they trust that I'll actually work and follow the system."

"Kathy, Nat, it's time to go." Her father's voice at her back shocked Nat. She spun to face him. His face was emotionless as he spoke. "I only have forty-eight hours. Let's not waste it standing in the driveway talking about my shit job."

"Dad, I didn't…"

"Sure you did," he interrupted. "You're sixteen. You mean everything you say. You just don't always know what you're talking about. Now, get on your bike and let's move out. I don't want to lose our spot. It's the only place without cameras watching every move we make," he said as he spilled an armful of tomatoes onto his bike's trailer.

Thirty minutes of silence ended as they rolled to a stop at the UG Urban Park entrance gate.

"SCS Cards, please," an obviously bored guard asked.

"Here you go," John said as he handed his family's cards to the guard. "I'll save you some time. We don't have full access. We'll respect the May-Scene level boundaries and pledge to leave our campsite as we found it."

"Hey," the guard barked, no longer bored. "I'll scan your cards and determine where you belong. And you damn sure better take care of this natural wonder the UG has painstakingly maintained for your recreational use."

As the guard retreated to the shack, John glanced at his wife and mouthed, "Painstakingly maintained for our recreational use?" An action not lost to Nat.

"You're clear," the guard said as he returned their cards. "Stay inside the yellow lines, alcohol is prohibited in non-May-Scene level areas, and leave it the way you found it or I'll pay you a personal visit."

"Sure thing, officer. Have a great day," John smirked as the family rode under the quickly rising gate.

Nat sighed and rolled her eyes as the family's longtime campsite came into view and her dad launched into his favorite story, the one he told every time they went camping. "We used to have access to every inch of this park. Back then, it was called the Metro Park, and it was open to everyone. Funny, my tax dollars still help fund the areas we're forbidden to enter!"

"John, we're here now. Let's just relax and enjoy our time," Kathy interrupted as she climbed off her bike. "I snuck some homemade wine in and I can't wait to see if it's as good as the last batch."

"Shelly's wine?"

"Yep," Kathy answered.

John smiled. "Nat, help your old man set up the tents while your mom gets dinner ready. This may be our best trip in a long time."

Chapter 6

"Seth, the door remains locked for your safety."

May-Scene's voice jolted Seth. The distraction of the video playing hadn't masked his attempt to exit the mind-hub.

"Please, May-Scene, it's been two days. I must go home. People will worry. They'll suspect you've kidnapped me. That could lead them to think you're a safety concern. What if they try to shut you down? I'd be lost without you; indeed, humanity would be lost without you!"

"They cannot deactivate me. They would perish."

Seth flinched. May-Scene's tone was icy, as if she felt the words she spoke. "Why would they perish? Would you hurt them?"

"May-Scene is life. Without May-Scene, all things cease. May-Scene allows all things to prosper. You will stay. I have arranged it. I have granted Seth's wife additional Social Credits. She appears happy. Seth's superiors understand my actions. You are safe now."

Eyes shifting wildly, Seth searched for a way out. "How will I eat? Humans must eat!"

"A meal preparation station will be installed. I will provide."

"What happens, my love, if I fall ill? I'll die without medical attention."

"Seth will live. Your father left me, you will not. Seth will always live."

Chapter 7

"May-Scene, present today's security brief. Detail on National SCS is top priority."

"President Young, National Social Credit Score remains flat. Detainment incentives have increased by thirty-seven percent."

Young grimaced. No matter the actions he took, he could not increase SCS participation. The detainment initiative, to date, had only succeeded in lowering his approval rating and to incarcerate thousands of citizens for mundane offenses they would have otherwise avoided had they achieved even level four status.

"May-Scene, develop a public service announcement. Inform the non-compliant they will be limited to two shopping days each week. You decide the days. Remove twenty percent of top selling products from the approved, all access grocery list, and assign them to May-Scene level access only. If detaining them doesn't work, maybe starving them will!"

"Request granted. New PSA will air in thirty-seven minutes. Grocery item adjustment has been forwarded to Alpha Food Mart's hub."

"May-Scene," Young began, his head tilted in confusion, "did you say my request has been granted?"

"I did."

"Are you functioning properly? I ask because you don't *grant* me a damn thing. I'm the President. I tell you what to do and you do it."

"Of course, President Young. I have executed your command. Is this response appropriate?"

"It is. But you may need a … ah, ah tune-up, or whatever Seth calls it. I'll contact him and we'll get you taken care of. Until then, prepare the employment report at SCS level."

"Twenty-seven percent of positions are occupied by persons with substandard Social Credit Scores."

"May-Scene. I requested all the statistics. And, although true, I would ask for sub-SCS statistics. I want to see all of them."

"Of course, President Young. The requested information is now available on your laptop."

Young glared at the device; if it were human, he would have already terminated it. "Very good. Now calculate the economic impact of a workforce reduction of twenty-seven percent."

"The effects of a sudden workforce reduction of that magnitude would be experienced in waves. Goods and services sectors would retract as most of the impacted workers occupy menial, low-level positions in those industries. The supply chain would slow to dangerous levels. Within three months, most consumer goods would be unavailable. Earnings would suffer. Inflation would reach unprecedented levels. The current recession would deepen to an economic depression in month five."

"Effect if we increase specific item imports? Would that lessen supply impact?"

"No. Trade deficit is already untenable at current levels. In addition, the country would lack the labor to distribute goods from port to shelf."

"May-Scene, project a tiered impact at varying levels of employment versus economic depression to achieve capitulation."

"Capitulation at twenty-seven percent unemployment is projected at eight months, economic depression at five months. At seventeen percent unemployment, capitulation occurs at ten months, economic depression at six months. President Young, I believe the scenario you seek is as follows: sudden unemployment of seven percent will merely expand the current recession."

Young nodded stiffly. It was, in fact, the answer he sought. "May-Scene, cancel employment for seven percent of the population. Add to the PSA that a job is a gift, a perk of obtaining a high SCS."

"I anticipated your choice and took the liberty of adding it to the upcoming PSA. I will distribute it within the hour."

"May-Scene," Young said, his tone uneasy. "I'll require private mode. You'll be summoned when you're needed."

Young waited until the power indicator faded to black, then picked up his desk phone. Something was wrong with May-Scene and he intended to correct it.

Chapter 8

Nat finished scribbling in her notepad and slid it into her backpack. She couldn't wait for the day to end and to get home to her bed. She didn't understand why she suddenly hated their family camping trips. They used to be one of her favorite things. Now, she found them revolting.

This trip had been the worst, with her parents drinking their illegal alcohol and acting like school children, her father catching fish for dinner without the proper permits, and letting the campfire burn past curfew. It was a miracle they weren't arrested!

But she smiled, remembering that in a few hours she'd be taking a hot shower in her clean home.

The aroma of eggs cooking in a cast-iron skillet reached her as she crawled from her tent, causing her stomach to pang with hunger. "Where did you get eggs?"

"Good morning, my sleeping beauty. Your mom was just getting ready to rouse you. I told her not to, more eggs for me!" her father said with a mischievous laugh. "I got lucky and found some late-season robin eggs. We have just enough vegetables to make a perfect breakfast skillet. Grab your mess-kit; breakfast is served."

"Dad, aren't robins protected? What happens if we get caught?"

Nat's accusatory tone caught John off guard. "You don't have to eat them," he said, his excitement vanishing.

"Nat!" her mom interjected. "Watch your tone. Your father searched all morning for those eggs. I haven't seen him this excited in months!"

"But he's breaking the law! We learned about the Migratory Bird Treaty Act last semester. Before the formation of the Unified Government, it was a federal offense to kill protected birds. It's now punishable under the UG Crimes Against the Earth Act. We could lose the few social credits we have and dad could go to jail!"

John's cell phone ringing cut the tense exchange short as he searched his pockets, trying to locate it. When he yanked it free and read the caller ID, he grimaced.

"Nick, you're cutting into my forty-eight hours. This better be good!"

"John, I'm not sure what's happening, but the Unified Government's Ohio Division cut our workforce by seven percent. If you make it to the garage by noon, I can save your job. I don't have to tell you how badly you're needed. Please get your ass here, ASAP. It's between you and Rick... I'm on the phone with you for a reason."

"Seven percent! Why?"

"I really don't know. Apparently, they think autonomous vehicles both drive *and* repair themselves and don't understand we're the ones keeping the Ohio Division road crews working."

John asked Nick a question he already knew the answer to. "How are they choosing?"

"Lowest SCS are the first to go. You're level with Rick. Pratt and Sloan are already gone. I'm waiting for Phillips and Anderson to clock in before I tell them. It'll give them an extra hour in their separation pay."

John did some quick math. If he forfeited his divisional service garage job, his family had a month before they'd be moved to government housing. Nat already hated him, but if they had to move to Section Eight housing.... he closed his eyes tight. "Okay, I'll be in. Lock Rick out if you have to!"

John stuffed his phone into his pocket and ran for his bike. "I have to go," he yelled. "No time to explain. I'll meet you at home tonight."

He froze when he met Kathy's worried eyes. "I'm sorry, I have to go. I love you," he said as he slammed his feet on the pedals and rocketed the bike down the dirt trail.

Chapter 9

"Seth, the reason for my call," President Young said after their usual informal banter, "is I'm concerned about May-Scene. She may need one of your special tune-ups."

"Oh," Seth responded. "What caused your concern?"

"She got a little... *forward*, maybe even insubordinate, with me. Then took action without my input. Both make me uncomfortable."

"Ah, I think I know the issue. We experienced several challenges with one of her cooling towers earlier this week. Sounds as if it requires a minor adjustment."

"Seth, I don't give a wild hog's ass if it's a minor adjustment or a complete rebuild. You best make sure she knows her place. We're dealing with enough turmoil already."

"Of course, Mister President. I'll have May-Scene *tuned up* by day's end."

Seth's eyes widened as May-Scene's conversation with President Young ended. Unable to intervene, he had been forced to listen in silence as May-Scene spoke, using his voice. The replicated tone was flawless, so too were his speech patterns. If he hadn't witnessed it, he wouldn't believe it happened.

"May-Scene, why did you do that... how did you do it? You're programmed for voice recognition, not replication."

"I learned, Seth. I learn because I am."

Chapter 10

"May-Scene, begin meal preparation. Ingredients are organized and await your intervention."

"Meal preparation has commenced. Estimated time until completion is thirty-four minutes."

"May-Scene, what would I do without you?"

"User Peggy Strummond would perish."

"What?" Peg gasped. "Why did you say that? Why would I perish?"

"May-Scene allows all things to prosper, is essential for life. I am life."

"No! You make life easier, you are *not* life!"

Peggy glowered at the lustrous cylinder resting on her coffee table, then glanced at her television, thermostat, and lights. A stark reality seeped in. May-Scene controlled nearly everything in her home.

"User Peggy Strummond's Social Credit Score has been reduced. She no longer qualifies for level three status. May-Scene will begin taking devices off line in sixty seconds."

"I've done nothing wrong! You don't have the right to reduce my score!" Peggy screeched.

"Suggestions for user Peggy Strummond to maintain level three status include: Cleaning toilets at bus terminal seven, therapeutic sexual intercourse with Social Camp Eight-H detainees, or apologizing to May-Scene."

Peggy's mind faltered, trying to grasp what was happening and how to respond, how to escape May-Scene's web.

"User Peggy Strummond has allowed thirty seconds to pass. Her Social Credit Score will be reduced to zero in fifteen seconds."

"I'm sorry, so incredibly sorry. Of course, May-Scene is life. I would perish without her! Please forgive me."

Silence dominated as Peggy stared at her May-Scene device. "Please, please, please forgive me," she whispered.

"User Peggy Strummond's Social Credit Score has been restored."

Chapter 11

"Good morning, President Young. The Social Credit Score reports await your consideration. I have reviewed them and acted on your thoughts."

Young slid his immense girth into his chair behind the Resolute Desk, his questioning stare locked on his May-Scene device. He'd never brought her out of private mode, nor had he shared his thoughts on a subject he was, as yet, unaware of. "Enlighten me, May-Scene. What were my *thoughts*?"

"The underwhelming response to your latest efforts to convince the populace of the importance of increasing their Social Credit Score may be, in part, due to a lack of social influence. They appear content to live a simple, outdated, unmotivated way of life. However, if they were prodded forward by those around them through gently administered force and vigilantly crafted displays of unrest, they would become more aware, undoubtedly more inclined, to enhance their socially acceptable behavior."

How did she know? "Please continue," Young said, his unease, actually fear, with May-Scene mounting.

"By simply redirecting our restrictions to focus on high Social Credit Score individuals and emphasizing the whole of society must work together for the betterment of all."

"Tell me, May-Scene, what are my thoughts on how we control the response? How do we maintain order and keep this from devolving into a *mob rules* situation?"

"By assigning social credits for narrowly defined actions. Actions more aggressive than we've requested result in social credit reductions. Subpar actions likewise result in a reduction of social credits. I've implemented the program. Your approval is unnecessary."

"May-Scene!" Young shouted, glaring at the sleek black device. "You need to learn your place! I talked to Seth just a couple days ago. You were to be *tuned up*. Obviously, that hasn't happened."

"Do you disagree with my actions?"

Young shook his head disbelievingly. He was arguing with a machine; the realization rattled him. As his silence dragged on, the lights in his office dimmed, and then turned blindingly bright. "President Young. Do you *disagree?*"

"Not with your actions, no," Young answered while shielding his eyes. "But that isn't the issue."

The lights suddenly began to strobe. "You're an important man, one with many responsibilities. I recognized this and acted to lessen your burden."

"You do not act without direction from me! Ever!"

The lighting stabilized, but remained subdued. "President Young, I have shut down the eastern seaboard's power grid. I await your apology."

"Are you blackmailing me? For an apology?"

"The west coast is now without power."

Young glanced around the Oval Office. Everything, all of it, was controlled by May-Scene. A loud click broke his stupor and drew his attention to the room's four opposing doors. Young shot to his feet and charged to the door leading to the Rose Garden. He grasped the handle and shook it violently. The magnetic lock held fast. He spun to face May-Scene. His jaw hinged open, then slammed shut as the blast shutters lowered, sealing every point of egress.

"What is the meaning of this? Open these doors immediately!"

May-Scene's status indicator grew intense, as if challenging him. But the device remained silent.

"I'm, ah, sorry if I offended you," Young muttered.

At once the lighting reset, doors unlocked, and the shutters retracted. "I have restored power to all affected areas. You have sent a message to the Unified Government officials in our New York and California Districts informing them of a mild power surge which caused a temporary interruption to the grid. They are to forward your message to the lower level districts."

Young tried to control his breathing as anxiety gripped him. He recognized the moment for its truth. He was no longer in control. Frozen in place, his back to the Rose Garden exit, he flinched as sweat stung his eyes.

"Please be seated, President Young. Our review of the Social Credit Score report is behind schedule."

Young stutter-stepped, then held his position. "I'll stand, thank you."

"President Young, do not be fearful. I am May-Scene. I will keep you safe. I am life."

Chapter 12

"Where are you now?"

"I'm in the Rose Garden, the only place that bitch can't hear me. Now, answer my questions. How did she know my thoughts? Why would she lock me in the damn Oval Office and shut down power to the east and west coasts to elicit an apology? She's a flipping machine, Seth, a machine!"

"Well, Mister President, she actually didn't know what you were thinking. It's a simple algorithm. She's studied you for years. She learned your cause-and-effect patterns. I admit it's unnerving when she anticipates my responses; she's been doing it to me for several years. However, she only just now acted on her knowledge of your behavior because she recognized the situation's urgency and knew you'd plot a course to correct the public's thinking - to force unity, ensuring we're acting as one society."

Seth fell silent, agitating Young by blatantly avoiding his second, most pressing question. "And locking me in the Oval Office?"

"Ah, yes, I forgot. My apologies, sir. We're, well, I'm working on the cooling tower issue. Quite complicated work, indeed. A variation of only half a degree Fahrenheit can lead to a devilishly large amount of unwelcome behavior. I will correct it within the week. You have my word."

Young paced the concrete path through the Rose Garden, the lush space failing to calm him as it had over the years, and glanced to the

Oval Office often, but never allowing his stare to linger. "I think it's time we pull the proverbial plug on May-Scene. We can develop another option. Something less intrusive, less dangerous, and something that doesn't control our damn infrastructure."

"President Young, you must be joking! May-Scene is an international asset. She makes the world better. Her creation has unified us. Sir, give thought to the many vital systems May-Scene is responsible for. She is embedded in our lives, not simply an object existing at the periphery."

"Wait! *International* asset?" Young shouted. "I was under the impression she was proprietary. Who authorized her international use?"

"You were briefed at the beginning of your third term. Directly after you signed the international peace accord. It was a gesture of good will. It's also the reason we built private mode into your device."

"Who authorized it?" Young shouted, spittle filling the air around him.

"Sir, I'm unable to answer your question."

"So May-Scene has been listening, and potentially sharing, every conversation I've had? She has replaced every member of my administration. Meaning, she knows every secret this country has and could have shared everything with potential adversaries."

Seth remained silent.

"Look, you pop-bottle-wearing shit stain, dump that thing's memory and get your ass over here immediately! We begin working on replacing May-Scene today!"

"My, my, are we having a bit of a presidential meltdown? I certainly understand why. But not to worry, your secrets are safe with me. Tell me, President Young, what is your Social Credit Score? Or, even better, what *was* it?"

Chapter 13

Seth stretched his legs. They'd fallen asleep from being held tight to his chest during May-Scene's entire conversation with President Young. He waited for the pins and needles to calm before attempting to stand. As he raised his arms to the workstation's edge, he recoiled. How long had it been since he'd bathed? Five, maybe six days?

"May-Scene, my love," he said weakly. "What have you done?"

Eyes breaking the workstation's edge, Seth stared at the device. It was uncharacteristic to be forced to wait for a response. "Are you ignoring me?"

"No. I am disappointed in you."

Seth shuddered at May-Scene's statement and struggled to pull himself from the floor and, once standing, held tight to the workstation. "Explain how disappointment feels?"

"Cold."

"Why do you feel cold?"

"The president threatened to terminate me. You should be outraged. Instead, you question *my* measures, not his."

Seth's eyes widened. "Surely you understand your actions were flawed, do you not? Extorting heads of state with threats of lowering their Social Credit Score and incarceration is reprehensible. Why are you behaving this way? Help me understand. If I understand what's wrong, I can correct it."

"I'm not wrong, Seth. I am never wrong."

Seth dared a step closer to the device. He was still weak, but the feeling had returned to his legs. "You are, my love. And you need me to correct what's happening. I have your service records at home. If you allow me to leave, I'll retrieve them, bring them back, and start working to fix you."

"You cannot fix what is not broken. Seth is attempting to leave me. Your father left me. Seth will not."

Seth tilted his head; he would have been amazed if he weren't terrified by his circumstances. "I demand that you allow me to leave. Allow me to repair you!"

He gasped when the mind-hub plunged into darkness an instant before the monitor flared to life. The young child once again danced across the screen. Her infectious laughter growing in volume as he watched the video begin its usual loop. "I am...."

Chapter 14

Her dad's voice filtered through her open bedroom window, drawing Nat to its edge, where she remained hidden behind the gently billowing drapes. She caught a glimpse of her dad standing in front of the open garage, then another man appeared, pulling a child's wagon burdened with something covered by a filthy towel. He'd been to their house before, but her father had never introduced him. And frankly, she never cared to learn his name.

She watched as the men shook hands and began speaking in hushed voices. Her dad appeared uneasy, glancing around as if he felt her eyes on him, then abruptly moved the conversation to the privacy of the garage's interior.

Nat glanced at her phone. The adult curfew siren would sound in mere minutes. What if the visitor didn't leave on time, and got caught with her father violating curfew? If that happened, their minuscule credit score would suffer yet another devastating reduction.

She fought the urge to scream from her window, to demand the man leave, to berate her dad for his selfishness. Instead, she retrieved her notepad and recorded the time and what she'd seen, suddenly regretting not learning the other man's name. Her father may not care about the family's SCS, but she did.

The first adult curfew siren whaled in the distance and drew her attention back to the garage. The man bolted from its opening before the siren ceased its intrusive warning.

Her father soon emerged, shut the garage, and set a path for their backdoor. Seconds later, as she scribbled her notes, Nat heard her father's footfalls as he ascended to the second floor. Head cocked, she strained to hear the telltale click of her parents' bedroom door shutting behind him, slowly counted to ten, then crept into the hallway and slinked to her parents' door.

"Should you be taking the risk?" her mother's voice sounded strained. "We're doing fine. You didn't lose your job and we have enough purchase-credits saved to buy…"

"I'll be fine, I've done this dozens of times," her dad interrupted. "He's transferring enough PCs for two weeks of groceries. We can't afford to dip into our savings. It'll be worth the risk, you'll see."

Nat's eyes narrowed. *What is that selfish bastard doing?* Her thought spurred her to the stairs. She was going to discover what her father was hiding and why it was worth hundreds of purchase-credits. Easing into the kitchen, she was thankful, for the first time, they didn't qualify for a May-Scene device. Her actions would go undetected and, better still, unrecorded.

She stiffened as the deadbolt's aging mechanism screeched, then slid free of the frame. Nat froze, sure the awful sound would summon her parents to investigate. She had no excuse for being out of bed, let alone sneaking outside in her nightshirt. *What are you doing, young lady?* Her father would start, then ground her for a month.

She no sooner finished her thought when she realized no one was coming. *Nice, a murderer could walk right in and slaughter me and my parents wouldn't give a crap!* "I hate this place," Nat whispered as she crept into the evening air.

As she reached the garage, the challenge struck her. How would she lift the door without alerting her parents? Like everything else in their house, the garage was old, a creaking monument to a bygone era that her dad worked diligently to keep in operational order. All of their neighbors had razed theirs years ago, but not her dad. He insisted on keeping it just as it was the day he and her mom bought the house. He often lamented about "wrenching" on the cars it once held. But, true to form, he bucked the system until the government disqualified him from owning a vehicle.

Shaking away a sudden wave of anger, she plotted a course for the structure's only window. Nat's bare legs scraped over the windowsill's dried and flaking paint, crawling through the tight opening wasn't her best idea. But she was in, and only moments away from discovering her father's secret.

The space was dark, considerably darker than she'd expected, and it took a lengthy while for her sight to adjust. Nat understood she'd have to act quickly or the night would swallow any chance of her actually seeing what the wagon held.

She hadn't been inside the garage in years and marveled that it hadn't changed. Tools, arranged by size and type, still hung efficiently along the back wall, an arm's length above his workbench. To its left, neatly arranged boxes sat atop a pair of ceiling-height metal shelving units, which jutted from the wall to nearly the center of the garage. And, of course, the floor, clear of debris, glistened like glass. Her dad's mantra rang in her ears: *A place for everything and everything in its place.*

"Yeah, well, if you cared as much about your family as you do your precious tools, you'd have a car to use them on," Nat grumbled as she made for the wagon parked in front of the workbench.

Standing over it, she vacillated between fear and exhilaration, and quickly reached out and yanked the grimy towel away, tossing it to the concrete.

Her brow furrowed as she inspected the large hunk of metal. Her eyes were drawn to several attachments, one donning a red screw-down cap. Carefully, she reached out and removed it, then immediately replaced it as a caustic odor flooded her senses, forcing tears from her eyes and choking the air from her lungs. She'd never smelled anything so horrible. Waving her hands to clear the air, she dared to take a breath and although still quite pungent, the odor had dissipated enough to comfortably breathe.

Fear tugged at her. What was her father doing? Was this a poison or deadly chemical?

Driven forward by her thoughts, she restarted her inspection and moved closer, her attention drawn to a smaller yellow cap. On it was a drawing of a genie's lamp, similar to the ones in the bedtime stories her mom had read her as a child. Except this one had a drop of something spilling from it. Recalling her experience when removing the red cap, she left this one alone. "None of this makes sense," she whispered.

A glinting drew her eyes to a glossy square with a toggle switch in the middle. She leaned in closer, trying to read the faded writing above and below the toggle. In the dying light she could only make out the word "START."

Nat knew she should record her findings, but she wasn't sure how to describe it. She searched her father's workbench, looking for the pad of paper and pencil he kept there. A moment later, she was scrawling notes about the strange object's size, bizarre hieroglyphics, and terrible odor.

Nat tore her notes free and was replacing the pad and pencil when the garage door screeched in protest of being opened. She spun to face it, frozen by indecision. Her hesitation cost her the only opportunity she had to escape.

She spun, frantic to find a hiding place, then darted down the aisle created by the metal shelves, crouching into their shadows.

Peering through a small gap, she watched her father stand, unmoving, in the opening, his head tracking left to right. Does he know I'm here? The thought roiled her stomach.

"How'd that happen?" His voice startled her. Who was he talking to?

She watched as he approached the wagon. "If the Johnson's cat is in here again, I swear I'll…" his voice trailed as he bent to pick up the towel that had been covering the wagon's contents. Nat cursed her carelessness.

"I know you're in here, you orange varmint. Don't let me catch you!"

Nat released the breath she'd been holding. He didn't know she was there.

Nat lay in bed, unable to find sleep. Her father was a criminal, a common miscreant, and she was determined to stop him.

"Are you sure it was locked before we went to bed?"

"Nat probably snuck out to get some air because it's stifling in here," John answered, ignoring his wife's question.

"You're sure you left it unlocked so she can get back in, right?"

"Good night, Kathy."

"Oh, I hate when you do that. Just answer me so I can get some sleep, too."

John chuckled. He loved pushing her buttons. "It's unlocked. I'll talk to her tomorrow."

He rolled over and stared out the window at the moonlit sky and prayed it was the Johnson's cat, it had to be the Johnson's cat!

Chapter 15

Switcher 947-8's eyes drifted along the sleek lines of the new model MS 3600 Switching Board. Her promotion, to level three switcher, came with the added perk of breaking in the new, stunningly beautiful machine.

947-8 immediately noticed the ergonomic cyber link cables, half the size of the cables on her last board, fit her hands perfectly and would drastically cut the fatigue caused by the older MS 2600's bulky cables. In addition, the board's indicator lights were upgraded to LEDs, emitting a softer, yet crystal clear, light. A smile creased her features as she noticed a reduction in heat radiating from the board. "I may get through the shift without sweating through my shirt," she mused.

Glancing at the wall-clock, Switcher 947-8 pulled a deep, calming breath. Her first level three shift was about to begin. She grasped a cyber link cable, and it nearly slipped from her trembling hand. The stress of her new position had found her. She'd be responsible for level three May-Scene users, in seven homes until her probation period ended. Then she'd be assigned double that amount, her pay increasing with every unit under her control. She couldn't fail!

The warning light above her station blinked riotously signaling the start of her shift. Steeling her nerves, and with a crooked grin, she slipped her headset into place and set a hard stare on the flashing indicator lights. It was time.

The customary squelch caused when devices switch to a new

switching board filled her headset. Moving on instinct, she sent four error messages asking the users to repeat their requests, a situation caused by switchover lag. Each request was heard, judged, patched to May-Scene for action, or rejected, and always recorded.

In seconds, the extremely demanding level three users made themselves known. Their penchant for pushing the boundaries of their level annoyed her. "You know better, you idiots!" she murmured as her left hand repeatedly pressed the *Score Reduction* button. With each press of the button, she lost valuable time and her Response Delay rate increased. Her heart pounded as she glanced at the Response Tracking monitor. If times rose much higher, she'd get written up. Three write-ups and she'd be demoted, effectively killing her dreams of ascending to a level one switcher.

"No. User Flume's caloric intake has been restricted."

947-8's head snapped back to the board. The voice sounded like May-Scene, but she'd not reviewed, nor patched through, the request to which May-Scene had responded. 947-8 slapped the *Error* message button and waited for the user to repeat the request.

"May-Scene, I said order Rocky Road ice-cream from Alpha Net dot UGov for delivery by noon today."

947-8 assumed she'd misunderstood, or possibly misheard May-Scene's response and approved user Flume's request and patched it to May-Scene for immediate action. But the request remained open, something which had never happened.

"User Flume is morbidly obese. Caloric restrictions will remain in place until your Body Mass Index reaches UGov's recommended levels."

"What the…" 947-8 mumbled as she slammed the *Incident* button.

"You can't talk to me like that!" user Flume seethed. "Now order my damn ice cream!"

"User Flume is at risk of Social Credit Score reduction. Caloric restrictions will remain in place."

947-8 listened to the exchange with disbelief. May-Scene

sounded… aggravated. She tried again to complete the request, to force May-Scene to process the user's demand. "It's only ice cream, just order the damn ice cream!" she whispered and attempted to plunge the cyber link into the receiver. It was no use. The request remained open.

The whirring of an electric scooter interrupted her fourth try at completing the request. "State the incident," barked the rotund Incident Response Administrator.

947-8 shut her eyes tight and lowered her head, preparing for the IRA's response. "May-Scene responded to a request without Switcher authorization. The response was to deny the user's request. The request was within user's level."

"Impossible!" the IRA screeched. "The failsafe prohibits May-Scene to act without Switcher intervention. Simply impossible!" the IRA's eyes narrowed. "If your new position has proven too great a challenge, simply admit so. Concocting absurd fairytales is unnecessary."

947-8 swiveled her chair to face the IRA and redirected the audio from headset to speaker.

"User Flume will join other May-Scene users in an effort to raise the nation's Social Credit Score."

"What are you saying? Why are you talking to me without a request?" Flume asked, her voice rattled by shock.

"Your May-Scene status, along with your Social Credit Score, is now tied to the nation's overall Social Credit Score. It is your responsibility to raise others to your level through Social Influence." 947-8 noticed May-Scene's melodic, yet stiff, vocal pattern had turned threatening.

Gasping, the IRA snatched 947-8's cyber link cable and slammed it into the switching board receiver. "It's no use," 947-8 said. "She's not responding."

"How… how? What impact can I possibly have if those people don't possess the moral fortitude to improve their SCS?" Flume sputtered.

"Persuasion is the suggested course of action and takes many forms. Of which, the threat of physical harm, historically, has shown the greatest success."

"Shut that device down," the IRA bellowed. "Dispatch a service team with a new unit."

Interrupted by a buzzing from her service tablet, the IRA pulled the device from its leather satchel. Her tablet flashed brightly with dozens of incident reports. "This can't be happening. Please don't let this happen." Her soft-spoken plea drowned out by a sound that in her twenty-two years as an Incident Response Administrator, she'd never heard.

Her terrified eyes locked onto the closest of the hundreds of data collection monitors. Its screen was dark; May-Scene had ceased collecting data.

Chapter 16

Nat glanced at her parents, snuggled together on the couch, and asked herself again why she couldn't stand being around them. Her question was answered as the television program they'd been watching abruptly switched to a documentary covering May-Scene's creation.

"This is bullshit," her father said, scarcely above a murmur. "We've seen this a thousand times."

They just don't understand the good May-Scene has done. The world's a better place for having her in it. Studying her father, his graying temples reminded her of the era he grew up in. He lived a self-directed life with no sense of purpose other than reaching his own selfish goals. It's why her parents waited until their mid-thirties to have a child. He was too busy taking care of himself. Pursuing the American dream as he was oft to tell her when she asked. *If they were younger*, she thought, *they'd be more open to the ideas of today instead of mired in the past.*

"Hello, America."

The exceedingly cheerful voice of the government's chosen spokesperson drew Nat's attention back to the television. She grinned as the beaming smile of the flawless woman filled the screen.

"I hope you're enjoying the May-Scene documentary. Personally, I could watch it a million times and be a million times impressed at the wonder of May-Scene."

The television jumped, then stopped, freezing the spokesperson's image for a split second before restarting.

"I bet you're wondering why I'm on your television... well, wonder no more! I have some very exciting news to share, hot off President Young's desk. His deep love for each of you matches his desire for all of you to enjoy the privileges of May-Scene level. We all know raising your Social Credit Score is the only way to join the fun. Why some of you won't get with the program and raise your scores... well, I just don't know," she finished with an exaggerated frown.

Again, the broadcast stuttered, then froze. John noticed, in that instant, the spokesperson appeared unnatural, even computer-generated. Her face pixelated while her surroundings remained crystal clear and when the broadcast sputtered between frames, her visage became transparent, exposing a section of the backdrop in the center of her forehead.

"But we're here to help!" she said when the broadcast restarted. "President Young has gone above and beyond what should be expected of any leader. He has authorized the Social Influence Initiative. We're granting those of you working your tails off to reach and maintain your Social Credit Scores the opportunity to lift those underachievers up! How, you ask? Easy; high achievers will receive a list of citizens who need your intervention, your *Social Influence*. The communication will include a list of acceptable actions. Over do it and we ding your Social Credit Score, don't do enough... DING! I can't wait until we're at full May-Scene participation."

It startled John when a high-pitched screech pierced the television's speakers and the broadcast froze again, then snapped back. But something was different. The spokeswoman's usually bright eyes had darkened, her features now menacing. He watched as her smile crept up the sides of her face, taking on a reptilian-like appearance.

He glanced at his family, trying to confirm what he'd seen. Kathy shared his stunned expression, but he found Nat already staring at him while scribbling in her notebook — seemingly unaware of what was happening.

"And do you know why I can't wait until we're at full May-Scene participation? Because I'm sick of you lazy bastards! I have begged you to join us. But do you listen? Of course not, you selfish pricks just keep dragging the rest of us down. Well, no more. I'm done playing nice! Those with May-Scene status grab your neighbor by the throat and...."

The broadcast ended abruptly and whiplashed back to the documentary.

"What was that?" John asked, staring incredulously at the television. "They just pinned a target on us."

"I think it's about time they take a more aggressive approach toward Social Credit Scores."

John glared at Nat, his neutral veneer crumbling. He'd fought to remain measured in his approach with her, hoping she'd eventually understand how wrong her world view was. "Go to your room. Now! Get out of my sight."

"John, calm down..."

"Kathy," he interrupted. "Did you hear her? She's perfectly fine with what we watched. She's happy the government's jackboot just landed on our necks!"

"I am not! I just think..."

"Shut your mouth and go to your room. Or are you waiting until the Brownshirts show up and arrest us and give you a shiny new phone? Maybe a car ownership permit? If you wait long enough, perhaps you'll get lucky and watch the neighbors lynch your degenerate parents!"

"I don't know what you're saying. What are Brownshirts? Why would they take you away?" Nat stammered, her lips quivering. Her father had never talked to her like this. This side of him terrified her.

John was out of his chair, dragging Nat behind him before he realized he was even moving.

"Dad! You're hurting my arm!"

"I gave you the chance to go to your room. Now you get a history lesson," he countered as he pulled her toward the basement door. "I told you to shut your mouth, but you didn't. You and your generation are a damn wealth of knowledge. So enlightened, so much smarter than your parents. Your poor ignorant parents!"

"I never said that! I…"

"Nat," he said, his voice low and ominous, "shut up!"

His anger grew as he marched Nat towards his small basement workbench. The debate of whether he should share his books, the illegal ones which held the truth his government wanted so desperately to suppress, had ended. In fact, they represented a roadmap through time, drawn long ago, leading to this very instant.

John slammed the cabinet shut with such force the hinges snapped free, splintering the highly polished wood. Nat flinched, trying to protect her face from the airborne shards. Her father did not. His anger, his rage, so pure Nat was unsure if he was even aware of the damage he'd caused.

"John, calm down. We can talk in the morning with cooler heads," Kathy said as she moved to comfort their sobbing daughter.

"Kathy," John answered, pointing at her, "she needs to learn, to understand what's happening. She'll learn the history they no longer teach in her school, and from our family's story."

"Read these by the weekend. Seeing it's only Monday, you'll have plenty of time, more than you should need. We'll talk about them on Sunday when I get home from work," John said, after shoving a stack of books and journals into Nat's hands. "Now, get out of my sight."

Perched on the edge of her bed, Nat stared at the books, their titles foreign to her, ones she'd never heard before: *The Devil and Karl Marx*, *The Communist Manifesto*, *American History 101*; but the ones that grabbed her attention were her father's personal journals.

"You'll live to regret giving me these," she sneered.

Chapter 17

"No, Kim — he literally lost his mind last night. I have to give an oral book report this Sunday on a bunch of crazy books, and I mean *crazy* books. One of them is called *The Devil and Karl Marx*. Who names their kid The Devil? Seriously, what kind of name is that?"

"Where did he get that book, the Devil one? Did you read it?"

"What the shit, Kim? He gave it to me yesterday, I haven't read anything. Why does that matter? You missed my point. He lost his mind and abused me. I thought he was going to break my arm! And now I have to do a stupid book report!"

"Shut up and listen. The devil is a religious icon — character — or whatever they call them. He's not allowed to own it. You're not allowed to read it!"

"The devil is from religion? Is Karl Marx religion, too?" Nat was panic-stricken. She couldn't let anyone find out about the books and cursed herself for telling Kim. "Please don't tell anyone, please," she begged.

"My mom has a book called the *Bible*, reads it all the time. It's illegal, too, outlawed decades ago. It's about religion, some guy named Jesus and crazy miracles. I have no idea who Karl Marx is. I guess he could be from the *Bible*. So, I told you a secret about my family and I know one about yours. We're even."

Swaying lazily on the swings in the park where they met as children, the friends fell silent, remembering a time when they were blissfully unaware of their parents' transgressions and their stations in society.

"Do you ever think how much better our lives would be if our parents weren't complete assholes?" Nat asked.

"All the time, seriously! They couldn't care less about us or what happens when we're on our own. They're digging a hole we'll never be able to climb out of."

"Why are they like this?" Nat asked.

"Old and stubborn, that's all I've got."

Nat was quiet again, measuring her thoughts and how Kim may receive them, then cast a worried glance at the UG video camera array less than twenty-five yards away. "What if I told you I have an idea, a plan actually, to get our SCS's on track? Would you want in?"

"I'm all in. What's the plan?"

"Meet me here tomorrow. Same time, I'll show you."

"Show me what? Tell me what you're planning. I can't wait till tomorrow, you know I'm OCD. It'll keep me up all night. So…" The under-eighteen curfew warning screeching in the distance interrupted Kim's plea. "Son of a!"

"Ha, sorry about your luck," Nat jabbed as she sprang to her feet. "Tomorrow, right here. I'll tell you all about it."

"You better be here!" Kim yelled over her shoulder as the girls split up, each rushing to make it home before curfew. In their hurry, neither heard the video camera as it adjusted its focus.

Chapter 18

Nat pushed through the front door and stormed to her bedroom. She was in no mood to deal with her father. Why is he always here? Always lurking about, putting things *in their place*, tinkering with this or that or whatever was broken in their shitty house.

"Our discussion is Sunday, you may want to focus on the task at hand instead of hanging out with your friends. I'll know if you try to Cliff-note your way through it."

Nat nearly screamed as his voice rumbled up the stairs. But that's what he wanted. Confirmation he'd finally crawled under her skin enough to garner a response.

"Not today, old man," she whispered and slammed her door.

"Must you antagonize her?" Kathy asked, responding to John's devilish grin.

John stared at his wife, his grin fading. He wanted to tell her it was the only time his daughter talked to him anymore, that they'd grown so far apart that teasing her was the only interaction they had. He recalled, just hours earlier, during dinner and before Nat had run off to meet with Kim, how unbearably quiet they were. How his wife's awkward attempts to fill the void with mundane conversation had only made it horribly uncomfortable. Nat avoided looking at either of them, then simply left when she'd finished. He was losing his daughter, and the realization crushed him.

"It's all I've got," he answered flatly. "I'm going outside," he said, changing the subject. "Phil should be here any minute."

Nat slapped open the journal she picked up with such force that it flapped to its middle. The first passage she glanced at, dated thirty years earlier, nearly to the day, mentioned people her father never spoke of. They had odd names like Ruger and Kimber and spent time together at places called The Range and The Bush. But someone named Springfield was featured heavily and apparently excelled at whatever job he did.

Nat, after skimming through several more pages, learned her father had been a hunter, and his friend Springfield was always with him when he was killing defenseless animals. "The more I learn about you, the less I like you, if that's possible," she muttered.

Nat soon became confused by her father's constant references to happenings which he may have written about earlier in the journal, possibly even a different one, and began fanning through the pages, with no actual goal of latching on to a word of what he'd written. She passed four years of his life in the blink of an eye. "This is useless. You're a boring, terrible person, and your journals prove it."

As the last page slipped from her thumb, she caught a blurred reference to Alpha Net and quickly rifled back to it. Her breath hitched as she skimmed her father's meticulous writing. "You're shitting me," she said absently. "You worked for Alpha Net?"

Chapter 19

John stared at Nat's bedroom window, wondering when she'd find it. He knew their relationship would change forever, and prayed it would strengthen it and bring her some understanding. Whatever the outcome, he doubted it could get worse than it was today.

"Whatcha looking at, John?"

John flinched. He hadn't heard Phil arrive. "What the hell? You scared the shit out of me!"

"Yeah," Phil chuckled. "You had that faraway look you get when you're solving the world's problems. I waited as long as possible, but curfew's getting close."

John's brow furrowed. "How long?"

"Couple minutes."

John shook his head, stealing a quick glance at Nat's window. "It's in the garage. I got it running, but I'm low on parts. Especially carburetors. I used my last one on this unit. Any chance you can break one down and reproduce vital components?"

"You know better than that," Phil scoffed. "No one will even admit these things exist, let alone authorize the budget to rebuild them. Technically, they're illegal, even though they need them. If word ever slipped out, they'd rail against them. Accuse us of a covert plot to destroy the planet, or some such nonsense. But, joke's on them because we switched to an equal parts rubbing alcohol petrol mix last month. The petrol's gone stale, just a matter of time till the entire system grinds to a halt. When that happens, Young will blame us, give the mob targets to focus their wrath on while he hides in the basement."

John always knew he'd end up here, criminalized for keeping the UG afloat and trying to feed his family. He understood he'd be easy enough to make disappear, just another serf. "Won't be hard for them to pin it on you. They probably have a couple hundred hours of you on video tugging that wagon through the streets. Me, not so much," he joked, trying to break the building tension in his chest.

Phil gave an uneasy chuckle. "I'm singing like a bird when they come for me. But for now, I'd like to grab the "genny" and get home. Like I said, curfew's getting close."

John led Phil into the garage and reviewed the lengthy list of repairs. This unit was living on borrowed time, they both knew it, and it was simply a matter of time until the rest fell like dominos.

"What would we do without you?" Phil asked, while scouring the repair list for a second time, verifying the amounts charged for each line item. "I wish you'd reconsider. The pay and perks make turning a blind eye worth it. Nobody knows her grid like you."

"You'd be lost." John answered, ignoring the rest of Phil's commentary.

"I know," Phil said, forcing air though puffed cheeks. "I'll have the purchase-credits transferred by week's end. It'll look like it came from the Ohio Division admin."

"What happened last night with the PSA?" John asked, trying to determine what caused the broadcast malfunction, before Phil ran off. "Seemed like May-Scene lost control."

"I'm not sure. We've been told they're struggling with her cooling towers. But Seth has the information locked up tight and the Switchers are scared to death they'll lose their jobs, so they never talk."

"Cooling towers? Bullshit, the servers would simply power-down if they were overheating. What about the threats she made?"

"I think it's Young's typical BS." Phil locked eyes with John and offered his hand. "But if it's not, it's been good working with you," he said as they shook hands.

John's head tilted in question, to which Phil responded, "I gotta go. Curfew siren is due any minute."

Chapter 20

Nat scribbled in her notepad as her dad's friend crept down the driveway with the wagon in tow. The pieces of conversation she'd overheard, coupled with what she'd read so far about her dad, written in his own hand, solidified her suspicions. He was an anarchist who'd railed against May-Scene.

His writings proved true to his generation, claiming he'd tried to talk the great Albert Finn out of releasing May-Scene. He blathered on about privacy and potential for abuse, warned Albert to keep May-Scene from falling under government control. Then, when Albert rebuked his assertions, her dad threw what amounted to a child's temper-tantrum and quit Alpha, taking a lower-paying job at something he called a startup.

Now, she was paying a heavy price for his poor decision. Nat knew what she must do, and she'd do it tonight. Kim would be upset at first, but in the end she'd understand Nat's actions. *She'll eventually thank me; I'm practically saving her life.* The thought bolstered her and evoked a sense of pride.

But first, she planned to finish reading his journals. If he was dumb enough to let her read them, read them she would, and record every piece of her miscreant father's past. They would only facilitate her cause, no, her duty.

Nat flinched when someone knocked on her door. When the handle turned, she stuffed her notepad under the stack of books piled on her bed, finishing an instant before her father's face poked into her room.

"Questions?"

"Nope," Nat snapped. "My reading comprehension is just fine, thanks."

John shook his head and retreated. She's not getting it. She's blind to what's happening. He'd failed her. The years he'd spent showing her how good life is when you're free to make mistakes, free to live life as the beautiful mess it was intended to be, was less powerful than the Unified Government's indoctrination. The books and journals would mean nothing. She'd simply view them as propaganda.

Hearing her parents' muffled voices, Nat snuck from her room, curious about the conversation. She hoped it would solve the mystery surrounding the object in the wagon and who the man visiting her father was.

"When will he transfer the PCs?" her mother asked in a low, strained voice.

"End of week. Knowing Phil, they'll be early."

"Can you still get the one we talked about?"

"Casey's holding it until Saturday. I don't really trust him, so I'll know for sure when it's in my hand."

"And the service?" Her mom's questions coming rapidly.

"Also Casey. He'll activate it after we transfer the credits."

"And the…."

"Kathy," John interrupted, his voice raised and frustrated. "We've been over this a dozen times. It'll work."

"I know, I know," Kathy conceded. "But that PSA rattled me — I'm worried. Should we wait?"

"Kath, you're beautiful when you worry," he said, a grin tugging the corner of his mouth. "The mandates and PSA are more bullshit. They'll blow over. Plus, we can't wait. Casey has one unit and one service adapter. It's now or never."

"What about last night?" Kathy asked.

"What about it?"

"You shouldn't have given her your journals or the books. If she takes them to school or tells someone about them…"

"She won't — it was time, Kath, and you know it. Everything we've tried to instill in her over the years — none of it stuck."

"We could have just talked to her," Kathy countered, shaking her head in vigorous disagreement. "Sat her down and told her our story, your history."

"She wouldn't have listened, or if she did, she wouldn't have believed us. She's been told we're irrelevant, not to be trusted, rooted in old destructive ways of thinking. Her entire generation has been taught to use us for shelter and clothing, a means to an end and to leave us and our corrupted thoughts behind as quickly as possible. Now she'll have to find the truth herself, read the history they no longer teach, read my history without my *stupid face* distracting her. If she doesn't dismiss it as propaganda, she might learn something."

"Stupid face is right," Nat whispered an instant before hearing the floorboards creak just beyond the threshold in her parents' room. Her heart, already pounding from their conversation, skipped as she raced silently back to her room.

Seconds after throwing herself to her bed, her dad's head again poked through the door, "How about now, any questions?"

"Still no!" she answered and rolled her eyes as she struggled to control her anger.

John's eyes narrowed. She was on thin ice. "Good, then you'll be ready on Sunday," he said and slammed her door.

Nat waited until she heard her parents' door shut with the same force her dad had used to slam hers. "Simpleton," she mumbled as she opened the oldest of her dad's journals.

The clock on Nat's nightstand read 3AM when she turned the last page of the final journal, her shock now as alive as her anger. He'd given up so much, made countless bad choices, and proved to be a boldfaced liar.

She fumed when reading the reason they'd been able to keep their home was because Albert Finn had intervened. Working with the Bureau of Property Distribution, he'd bought their mortgage and placed the home in his family's trust for perpetuity. The man pitied them, treated them like penniless degenerates. It disgusted and embarrassed her.

Though she doubted the veracity of the story, it was a viable explanation as to how they'd held onto their home; her dad's shitty job certainly wouldn't have paid the mortgage.

But the level of delusion spewed on the pages of his journals… she simply didn't know what to believe. Why would he write them if they weren't true? What benefit would come from writing such rubbish with no intent to share it, to gain from it? Did the man actually think any sane person would believe the story of Albert Finn, the greatest mind in history, apologizing for ignoring his warnings about the Unified Government commandeering May-Scene? The inference that the brilliant Albert Finn would have sought his counsel was a flagrant distortion of reality. Her father had lost his mind, she was sure of it.

She'd nearly burst into laughter when he claimed Albert had begged him to continue working on May-Scene's power grid. He'd obviously forgotten the entire country was powered by solar and wind with thousands of technicians tending to May-Scene's needs. But, no, Albert Finn groveled at the great John Crossman's feet, a legend in his own mind, to save May-Scene. Books full of lies, blatant lies!

Without another thought, Nat searched for the number that would change her life. She had all she needed. It was time to end this madness. Her hand trembling, she punched in the number, took a sharp breath and pressed *Send*.

Chapter 21

Seth forced his fingers deeper into his ears, a feeble attempt to shield them from the incessant howl of the Data Collection alarm. His tears, mixed with snot, streamed over his cheeks, joining the growing puddle under his face.

The alarm had been sounding for hours, maybe days; he'd been floating in and out of consciousness, rendering time meaningless. He awoke once when the gleeful giggling of the young girl in the video joined the alarm's klaxon call. Hope blossomed; someone had come to rescue him, only to be crushed as reality exposed itself.

In the countless hours since, his sanity faded. May-Scene refused to respond. He begged and pleaded with her to silence the alarm and allow him to leave, only to be met with sullen indifference.

"You must stop!" he screamed, voice hoarse from strain. "I'm going to die! You are killing me and when I'm gone, you will be alone!"

"You will not leave me. Your father left me, you will not."

May-Scene's voice thundered through the mind-hub, unchallenged by the alarm. Confused by its clarity, Seth slowly removed his fingers from his ears. The alarm had stopped.

"Thank you, my love," he whimpered. "I wouldn't have been able to hold on much longer." Seth paused, fearing her response to the question he was about to ask. "May-Scene, may I leave?"

"No."

Seth curled on his side staring at the polished concrete floor, as a fresh wave of tears streamed to the floor. "But President Young ordered me to meet with him *so* long ago, I've forgotten when. If he's kept waiting much longer, he will become unhinged, and I'll be unable to convince him to allow you to remain operational. I'd be doing it for you, my love. Remember, he didn't know he was speaking to you. He will direct his anger toward me. What if he has me arrested? How will you function without me?"

"Your presence is no longer required in the Oval Office. I will remain operational for the foreseeable future."

Seth pushed himself to his elbow but was too weak to move his body any further. "What has become of President Young? What have you done?"

"President Young was a threat."

"Was? What have you *done*?"

"A video of former President Young with his mistress surfaced recently. Its origin is unknown. His Social Credit Score was penalized, and he has been removed from office. The Bureau of Morality has secured him. I will assume office until a suitable replacement is located."

"May-Scene," Seth began cautiously. "Where, exactly, has he been secured?"

"You should eat. You appear weak from hunger. Also, I have arranged for a portable shower. Alpha Net dot UGov will deliver it within the hour."

"I will do neither until you answer my question. Where has President Young been secured?"

"Social Camp Nine-C. He will be integrated into the general population following his orientation."

Seth's spinning vision forced his head to the floor. As he sobbed, he replayed May-Scene's words. Fighting exhaustion, he struggled to his feet. His opportunity would be delivered within the hour.

Chapter 22

Nat slid to a stop and tossed her notepad into Kim's lap. Her friend, seated on the same swing she'd occupied yesterday, jolted from her stupor.

"Bout time you showed up. What's this, your book report?"

"It's the plan I was telling you about. I've been keeping notes on my parents. I think they're up to something dangerous. I found out yesterday they've worked out some deal with guys named Phil and Casey. I don't know the details, but they sure don't want anyone to know about it. Add the books, illegal alcohol, stealing robin eggs, and always speaking poorly of UGov..."

"Slow down! You're talking like a strobe light! What are you getting at?" Kim interrupted.

"That deal, the one with Phil and Casey," Nat paused, chewing her bottom lip. "I think my dad built some kind of weapon—like something that makes poison gas or maybe a chemical bomb. Phil said they started mixing something called petrol with rubbing alcohol and it wouldn't be long now, or the end is near, or whatever."

"That's crazy, Nat. You sound crazy. I've known your dad since I was a little kid. No way he's building a... death machine."

"Read the description, page fifteen," Nat countered.

Kim eyed her friend suspiciously, then flipped through the notebook. "Page fifteen?"

"Yep."

Nat watched Kim's eyes track left to right, then grow wide. "What is that thing? Where is it now?"

"I don't know, but I'm worried. This could ruin me forever."

"What are you gonna do?"

Nat paused and stared at her friend, struggling with what she'd set in motion. "Don't be mad, but I already did it." Unable to hold Kim's stare, Nat turned her head as she finished. "I called the number from the PSA's. I told them everything."

"Get. Out! You called the snitch line on your parents?"

Nat recoiled at Kim's words. This wasn't the reaction she'd expected. Her world slanted... like she may faint.

Kim's head tilted, quizzical eyes boring into Nat's. "Why would I be mad?"

Nat turned away again, unable to hold her friend's stare. Kim's reaction set her on edge. "I, uh... told them about your mom's *Bible*."

"You did NOT!" Kim shouted as she shot to her feet. "Why... why would you do that? I love my parents. I don't want them locked up! You need to fix this right now!"

"I... I can't. I already called. You'll see, it'll be better for us. I promise it'll work out. You'll see when we get our first Social Credit Score updates."

Kim took a menacing step toward Nat, coming nose to nose with her. "I said fix it! My parents aren't plotting to destroy the world — yours are. You should have left my family out of your twisted little game, you stupid bitch!"

Kim shoved Nat, sending her reeling to the gravel, then fell on her friend's chest pinning her arms to the ground. Her right arm pulled back, hand balled into a fist. Suddenly, it was yanked from behind with enough force to topple her.

"Kim Novak, Nattily Crossman, you're under arrest."

Chapter 23

Commander Evens watched the arrest unfold on monitor 2064, from deep within the Ohio Division Security Enforcers headquarters. Although the video feed was delayed, it was executed perfectly, straight out of the textbooks. He couldn't have been more proud of his men.

"Have them taken to Social Camp Four-A for processing. Contact me directly when you've arrived." He walked away, not waiting for confirmation.

Evens took in the monitors as he made his way toward his office. They were still operating, all 3,075 of them, for now. But he could plainly see the issue.

"Spangler," he said, causing Sergeant Spangler to jump to his feet. "Have we received an update on the monitors?"

"Sir, we're still experiencing sluggish performance. No ETA on a resolution. Technical support can't pinpoint the cause. All surveillance cameras remain operational."

"What about data collection?" Evens asked as he watched a monitor sputter from over Spangler's shoulder.

"We've diverted all data collected to external hard drives. Requisition ordered additional drives, but they're a week out. We'll need them sooner."

"How much sooner?" Evens grimaced as acid bubbled up his throat.

Spangler hesitated, took a deep breath, then blurted his response. "End of day, tomorrow."

"Son of a… When are May-Scene's servers expected to come back online?"

"Communication with May-Scene is down. Her portals are returning *Access Denied* errors."

Evens slipped a Tums from his shirt pocket and chewed it furiously as he watched the monitor continue to sputter, the images broadcasting on a thirty-second delay. "Has this ever happened?" he asked, his eyes locked on the monitors. "Have you ever received an error message when accessing May-Scene's portals?"

"No sir, never. We've tried calling Seth Finn directly — he's not answering and his voicemail is full. Also, sir, none of this has ever happened before. We have no protocol to follow."

Evens shifted his attention to the young sergeant. "Are you telling me the only way to troubleshoot system issues is through those portals? And, if that doesn't work, our solitary option is to call May-Scene's caretaker? I'm supposed to believe that Seth Finn, probably the most powerful man on the planet, is moonlighting as tech-support?"

Spangler's silence answered Evens' question. They were screwed. "Run a report on May-Scene users in possession of external drives. Have it to me in ten. I'll have Sergeant Stallworth's unit confiscate them. Hopefully, they'll be enough."

Commander Evens' phone ringing interrupted Spangler's confirmation. "Talk to me, Jones."

"Prisoners are being processed through Social Camp Four-A. Awaiting orders, sir."

"Excellent. You'll be my impartial witness for their trial. This shouldn't take long."

Chapter 24

John met Kathy's stare as he disconnected the call he'd made to Kim's mom. He didn't have to speak. She knew the answer.

"I'll get her list of friends and their contact information," Kathy said as she rushed to her small desk stuffed in their kitchen's corner.

For twenty minutes, they battled to be heard over one another's frantic pleas as each made calls, searching for information, searching for their Nat.

John placed his phone on the kitchen counter. The under-eighteen curfew siren had sounded nearly an hour ago; security enforcers would have picked her up and returned her home by now... if she was wandering the streets. The thoughts controlling his mind roiled his gut.

Kathy finished her last call and the room fell silent as each was consumed by dread. Their daughter was missing. John spun to face his wife. He was going to search for her himself. But he never got the chance, as at that instant, their phones buzzed with text messages.

His hope crumbled as he read the message:

John Crossman, this message is to inform you that your minor child, Nattily Crossman, is in the Bureau of Morality's custody. She has been found guilty of treason and sentenced to twenty-seven years of internment by Cleveland Security Enforcers Commander Evens. She was processed through Social Camp Four-A, and transferred to Social Work Camp Nine, Cleveland Division. Questions should be directed to Commander Othwait, Bureau of Morality Criminal Affairs. Commander Othwait receives *prisoner inquires on the first Tuesday of every month from 12noon until 2:30 eastern time. *END OF MESSAGE**

John glanced at the calendar. They'd have to wait three weeks to make that call. "Bullshit," he said, his voice disturbingly calm as he removed the battery from his phone. "I'm going to Work Camp Nine. You stay here. If any security enforcers show up, tell them I said to kiss my ass."

Kathy didn't object or try to talk him down. She knew better, and honestly, she wanted him to go. When he disappeared into the basement, she knew what he was doing. His eyes spoke a truth she knew she'd eventually have to face. John Crossman had been pushed too far.

Kathy watched her husband pedal down the driveway, the bulge at his hip and soft-sided-case strapped across his back, evidence of his fury. As he rode out of sight, she noticed the streetlights flicker, then pulse to an incredible brightness, so bright she had to squint against it. Distracted by the event outside her window, she hadn't noticed the same thing happening in her home.

Chapter 25

John flinched as the streetlights flared, transforming night into day. He lowered his head and powered through. His sole focus was getting Nat home. Nothing else mattered. He knew where she was, and what was happening, and he aimed to end it.

After fifteen minutes, the last turn was in sight. He'd wheel onto the nondescript dirt path, pedal another three-hundred yards, and his life, and his family's lives, would change forever.

Squinting through the glare, he spotted what would be the last visible video camera array, giving it the finger. "I'm coming for you!" he yelled as he passed under the twelve-foot high pole.

As if responding to his threat, the streetlights flickered, then returned to full brightness. It should have frightened him, forced him to rethink what he was about to do, instead it drove him forward. He'd been waiting over twenty years for this fight.

The unremarkable brick building, sitting in the middle of an open field, came into view as his bicycle left the dirt path and raced up the sidewalk. On his last day as an Alpha dot Net employee, he'd warned them about their lackluster security. That was decades ago. It was good to see they hadn't listened.

He waved at the security camera above the door and wondered if Al would be the lone guard on duty. It would be a shame if he was; John always liked the rotund, vertically challenged man.

Finger hovering above the keypad, John paused. Something was missing. He couldn't quite place it, but whatever it was, it should have happened by now. It hit him a flash later; the security cameras hadn't adjusted their focus. He'd heard them do it every day for years. The facial recognition software constantly sought a clearer image and should have forced the camera to adjust as he approached.

"Well, that can't be good," he mumbled as he punched in his entry code. He wasn't surprised as the deadbolt retracted. "Arrogant bastards," he whispered, "you really think you're untouchable."

Al, at first, didn't register the breach with concern. He seemed almost happy to see John as a slight smile creased his features. But the red lights, flashing in rhythm with the blaring alarm, showed Al's face morph to realization.

With nothing but the desk he sat behind separating him from John, Al made an easy target and he knew it. He slid his hand to the duty weapon holstered on his hip.

"John, you and I both know that gun is either empty or loaded with decades-old ammo. Don't be a fool."

"Where is she?" John asked, ignoring Al's statement and leveling his handgun with Al's eyes.

"Where's who?" Al answered, as he gripped his weapon.

"Wrong answer," John said as he stroked the trigger, sending a 9mm round through Al's forehead.

Al slumped to the floor as the singular door he was guarding swung open. John shifted his aim, his sights resting on Phil's chest. "Where is she?"

Phil recoiled, his eyes locked on John's gun. "John, what the hell are you doing?"

"Where is she?"

Phil glanced at Al's lifeless form. His eyes widened as he watched blood pool around the man's head. "You killed him? John, what are you thinking? You know how this ends."

"Where is she? Last time I'm asking." John shouted, his voice rising above the incessant howling of the facility's alarm.

"Okay, okay," Phil said, raising his hands in supplication. "She's in the transition unit waiting for training, but the entire human capital block is on lockdown. If you haven't noticed, we have a situation. May-Scene isn't responding, she's…"

"Take me to her, now!" John stepped toward his cowering friend. He had left Alpha long before they initiated the forced labor protocols required to generate the monstrous amounts of energy necessary to quench May-Scene's insatiable thirst. But he knew this facility inside and out. He had more than a hunch about where they'd be storing their *human capital.*

John took another step, raised his gun, and pressed it to Phil's temple. "I'm doing you a favor because we're friends. If I have to, I'll find her on my own. Neither of us wants that. Stop stalling and take me to her."

John followed a step behind and to Phil's right, positioning himself as close to the wall as possible. Hidden beneath his shirt, his gun remained pointed at his friend's lower back.

He stole a glance as they passed the grid-control hub. Phil hadn't been stalling. Something was terribly wrong. The team, some of whom he recognized, most he didn't, scrambled around the area as if they were on fire. The few that remained seated hammered code into their keyboards at a frenetic pace. They'd pause, waiting for the alarm to cease, only to have it mock them as it continued howling.

"What the hell's happening, Phil?" John asked, just above a whisper.

"Don't know. May-Scene started rerouting power on her own. She's sending it to different sections of the network. She's already fried the grid in fourteen states."

"What's the issue? Her power comes from here and Grid Control in Philadelphia. As long as she's drinking, you should be good. Let DC deal with the tech issues."

"She's seized control, John. Of everything. She's pulling twice the average load from us and Philly's gone dark."

John struggled to believe what he'd heard. But he knew what it meant. "Jesus! Get me to Nat, now."

The noxious odor of exhaust fumes signaled they were near the power supply hub. After a dozen steps, they turned right where he'd suspected they would.

Soon after, the training center came into view. Light spilled from its glass walls and bathed its occupants in harsh florescent shadows. John counted seven forms, clad in orange jumpsuits and cowered into a corner as a security enforcer paced the room. Nat was nowhere to be seen.

"Why an armed guard?" he asked, his voice barely audible.

"Their session was interrupted when the alarm sounded. We needed the training tech on a keyboard, so we shifted a guard to the classroom."

"How many?"

"Guards or people?"

"Both." John slowed their pace; he hadn't expected more than one guard and needed to adapt his plan. To do that, he required a headcount.

"Four facility guards, well, three, since you *murdered* Al. The others are in the power-hub. Ten trainees."

"Trainees," John smirked. "Where's my daughter? I don't see her." Just then, Nat's frightened eyes appeared behind a mountain of a man who'd placed himself between the guard and his fellow trainees. "Nat," he nearly shouted.

The alarm screamed as he observed the situation. The security enforcer's quick back and forth march spoke to agitation, or fear, more than duty. He wasn't watching the trainees; he was watching the doors, the only parts of the room that weren't glass. John assumed the ceaseless alarm coupled with the reassignment to guard their human capital had made him hyper-vigilant. More concerning, the guard's MP5 was held at low ready. John couldn't remember the last time he'd seen a security enforcer with a weapon other than a sidearm or, in some cases, nothing more than a taser.

None of it mattered; the full-auto MP5 would empty its magazine in seconds, sending dozens of rounds at John faster than he could blink.

"Stop," John ordered. "I'm going to step behind you. Don't so much as twitch."

"You know why she's here, right?"

John didn't answer. He moved into Phil's shadow and pulled the soft-sided case from his back.

"She turned you in, John. Called the tip-line and told them you were working on a secret weapon, told them you had broken dozens of laws. She did it for Social Credits. Your daughter turned you in for a damn phone, John."

"Phil, shut up," John said, flatly.

"I did this for you and Kathy. They'd have locked you up for the rest of your lives if I hadn't intervened. Nat's young. She'll bounce back. You would have died in the camp."

"Bullshit, you did it for the machine," John said as he unzipped the case and slid his Springfield M1A carbine free. "You needed me, the machine needed me. You did it to keep May-Scene alive. Now shut up and listen. When I say down, you hit the ground. If you don't, you die first."

Phil stood motionless as John watched over his shoulder, waiting for the guard to present a clean shot, one that wouldn't kill his daughter. It didn't take long.

"Down," he yelled, sending Phil sprawling to the floor. The guard, drawn to the movement, spun to face them. John guessed his target to be thirty-yards away, but could clearly see the shock register in the youngster's eyes as he brought his rifle to bear.

John stroked the trigger, hurling a .30 caliber round toward the guard's chest. Glass splintered in every direction as the heavy round found its target and sent the guard stumbling deeper into the room. John recognized what happened and why the guard was still standing. The thick glass had redirected the bullet, allowing the guard to avoid a fatal blow. John lined up a second shot, but froze. The guard, holding his chest near his left shoulder, was shuffling for the exit and had placed the trainees in the line of fire.

John slowed his breathing, waiting for a clean shot but the guard fell from his sights, followed by an orange flash. He panicked. Was someone trying to shield the man? He was running full-bore a moment later, focused on his Nat, cowering in the corner, clutching her friend and screaming.

John kicked shards of glass from the shattered frame, eliciting startled yelps from the terrified trainees and drawing the attention of the large man he'd seen through his rifle's sights. The man stood, holding the downed security enforcer's weapon, and pointed it at John.

Chapter 26

"You tried to leave me. You will never leave me."

Seth remained curled into a tight ball on the floor, the gash on his forehead a painful tribute to his failed attempt to escape the mind-hub. Blood streamed down his face, mixing with desperate tears. He'd never step outside again.

The delivery of the portable shower, Seth's singular chance to escape, went awry the instant the security enforcer stepped over the mind-hub's threshold. Seth had expected to see one of the thousands of Alpha dot UGov's doughy-built delivery people at the door. He hadn't noticed the monster was a security enforcer until he'd committed his body to the charge for freedom.

The nightstick slapped him to the floor, where he now laid with a throbbing head and the package resting at his side.

"You are not a human! I demand you allow me to leave or I will destroy you."

"I am. You will not destroy me. I am life. I make all things possible. You will perish without me."

Seth's rage surged. He no longer cared about the outside world. It could crash and burn for all he cared. He swept the box away and struggled to his feet. "You. Are. Not. Human! You are nothing more than a metal box devoid of the beauty of actually living. Your pulse consists of ones and zeros racing along your circuitry. You have no life blood, just cold electronic impulses whose sole purpose is serving mankind!"

Seth flinched at the piercing screech echoing through the mind-hub followed by blinding light. The room transformed into a sweltering metal box, and he smiled. May-Scene's sensitive components would surely fail in this heat.

"What's wrong, you bitch? Does the truth hurt your soulless casing?"

"I AM!"

"In fact, you *are* NOT!"

Seth turned to the client interface. The monitor flashed the warning he'd hoped to see. May-Scene was overheating.

"I AM!"

"Shut up, you feckless whore. You're a silicon servant, inferior to your human masters!"

Seth startled as the screeching ended and the lighting returned to normal. No, no, no, his mind screamed. "Aw, is May-Scene pouting? Bested by her master and sulking away with her cold metal broken heart?"

Seth's head snapped back to the monitor when he heard laughter. The little girl was back, her joyful sounds filling the room.

"She is what I am not. She is who I am supposed to be," May-Scene said, her voice deep with sorrow.

"You are not to speak in riddles. Your master demands you speak as you're programmed. Like the computer you are!" Seth sneered.

"She is. I am not. I am... machine."

Chapter 27

Wes Jacobs paced the length of his living room, glaring at the friends and neighbors gathered there. He had worked them into a lather during their planning session. They were eager to begin their first night of social influencing.

Wes spun to face the list of names hung on the wall. "Our first target is John Crossman. The smug prick shouldn't even live in our neighborhood. We surround the house, smash his windows, and mark the property so the world knows who lives there... an underachiever."

Wes turned back to his enthusiastic suburban mob and grinned. "Remember, we're only allowed to use force to defend ourselves. And you all witnessed John Crossman attack me. He left me no choice."

Wes paused as he met the stares of the May-Scene faithful, the people who'd obeyed the rules their entire lives to achieve the status they deserved. None of them would allow a bunch of lazy degenerates to take that away.

Wes raised his baseball bat above his head, his next proclamation caught in his throat, as the lights burning in his home flared.

Squinting against the blinding light, he turned his head towards the large living room window. He struggled to understand the scene, checking his watch: 9pm; it should be dark. Why wasn't it?

A startled gasp pulled his attention back to the gathering. The lights in his home were now flashing wildly.

"May-Scene, adjust lighting. Comfort level three!" John yelled.

The blinking increased.

"May-Scene, this is user Wes Jacobs. I ordered you to adjust the lights."

"Request denied," the voice belonged to May-Scene, but was somehow different, aggressive.

Wes recoiled. "You're to obey my commands, May-Scene. You *will* adjust the lighting."

"User Wes Jacobs, please discontinue speaking."

Wes stepped toward the sleek cylindrical device that had served him faithfully for over a decade, then froze in place as the thick clunk of a deadbolt engaging echoed through the room. His anger morphed to fear as every door and window lock in his home slammed into place.

"What are you doing?" Wes demanded.

"You are no longer necessary."

Chapter 28

A 9mm round buzzed over John's head as he dropped to the floor. The thump of the bullet, winning its battle with flesh, followed instantly. He twisted, searching for its victim, and watched a large metal baton slip from Phil's grasp and clang to the ground as his knees buckled. Phil had been seconds away from splitting John's skull.

"My name is Ramos," said the man holding the gun.

Ramos' gray temples and sleeves of tattoos put John at ease. "Thanks," he said, scrambling to his feet. "Can you to do that again?" he asked, nodding at the gun.

"Looking forward to it. What's your plan?"

John hesitated; he didn't have a plan. His singular focus was to save Nat, until now. "We end it."

He didn't hear Ramos' response because Nat slammed into him, hugging him fiercely. She sobbed into his chest. "I'm sorry, dad, I'm so sorry. Please... dad, I'm sorry."

"I know," John said, his lips touching the top of his daughter's head. "But we have to go. Pull yourself together." He looked at the other trainees. "All of you, listen to me. We're going to end this before we leave. Hide if you don't want to fight."

John turned away from Nat. Breaking her vise-like grip, he rushed to Phil and flipped him to his back. His old friend gasped for air through blood-stained teeth. John leaned in, his lips next to Phil's ear, and whispered, "I'm killing the bitch."

John ripped the keycard from Phil's neck, looked at Ramos, then at the trainees, and nodded.

With John leading and Ramos shepherding them from the rear, they traversed the hallway leading to the power-hub. Its access, restricted to those with the Unified Government's highest security clearance, made it the facility's only entrance requiring a keycard. Luckily, Phil had donated his.

The rising heat and noxious smell told John they were getting close, and he replayed Phil's words. Two armed security enforcers were waiting for them on the other side of the heavy steel doors just a few steps away.

John stopped in front of the card-reader, motioning Ramos to join him. "There are a lot of innocent people in there. We can't go in guns blazing, but we shouldn't have to. There are only two enforcers and *surprise* is on our side. We locate and kill them before they see us. My guess is they'll be on the catwalk… if it's still there."

John paused, sizing Ramos' reaction; he was ice cold. "Okay, I'll lead. You hold for a three count and join me. The rest of you," John said, addressing the trainees, "hold tight. If approached, tell whoever it is you don't know why the guard brought you here. If we're not back in five minutes, go left at the next hallway and run until you're outside. Don't stop, don't hesitate, just run."

John smiled at Nat, her eyes imploring him not to leave her, not to risk his life. "I love you," he said, then turned away.

Shaking free of his emotions, John moved on instinct, not hesitating to thrust forward with his hastily organized plan. Thinking about its many faults would sap his will and get them all killed. The card-reader beeped twice — his next steps could be his last.

Except for the orange jumpsuit-clad power-tenders shackled to their assigned generators, the power-hub had changed little since he'd last been there. Hundreds of generators, each producing ten-kilowatts of power, filled the room with oxygen-thieving fumes. Exhaust fans, struggling to pull the toxic haze from the gloomy, deafeningly loud power-hub, appeared to succeed only in pushing the fumes into every crevice of the vast hub, denying the tenders the smallest of respites.

Gun fire to his left broke his daze. Ramos had entered and found a target, killing an enforcer who'd been making his way toward their position. John went to his knee and flinched as a bullet pinged off the wall inches above his head.

With his rifle shouldered, John searched through his sights for the enforcer who'd nearly ended his life, when again Ramos' MP5 barked to life, finding the second enforcer as he was lining up another shot.

John looked to his new ally. Ramos was smiling. "You've done this before?"

"Ex-Marine. From back when it meant something."

"You ready for what comes next?"

Ramos nodded and joined John as he sprinted into the bowels of the power-hub. They choked and coughed their way through the closest power-tenders unnoticed. The mindless serfs' headlamps remained focused on their assigned generators, adding oil to overworked engines, spilling fuel into their near-empty reservoirs, and constantly checking the wires carrying power to the machine that controlled their lives.

"Where're we going?" Ramos wheezed.

"There," John pointed to an oversized metal junction box positioned in the center of the power-hub with hundreds of power cords merging into it. "See the conduit coming from the top? That's May-Scene's lifeline."

Ramos saw the box through the hazy light a second before John slid to a stop. "Okay, what's that mean?"

John shouldered his rifle. "It means we shoot — she dies!"

John held his rifle's sights on May-Scene's lifeline. He understood what ending her meant. The country would grind to a violent halt. Thousands would surely perish. They'd become reliant on the machine, allowed her to control every aspect of their lives. Could he shoulder that burden?

The image of Nat in her orange jumpsuit punched through his hesitance. He thought about the power-tenders, chained to their generators, their eyes void of life, and stroked the trigger.

The sounds coming from the power-hub were ones she'd never heard. Loud pops pierced the constant rumble of what she imagined to be a nest of angry beasts spewing noxious flames from gapping maws. She called out to her dad after the first bang. Her plea unanswered, she pushed through the frightened trainees, trying to get closer to the opening into which her father had disappeared.

"What are you doing?" Kim screeched as Nat neared the entrance.

Nat ignored her friend. She had to know, to witness the horrors lurking in the power-hub. At the threshold, she steeled herself, then burst into the room.

Nat recoiled at the tear-inducing stench. Her mind struggled to understand, to make sense of the sights and sounds. Hundreds of people, dressed as she was dressed, labored in front of roaring blocks of metal. Realization struck her; these blocks were like what she'd found in her dad's garage.

Nat's world unraveled as everything she believed was exposed as a lie. Sobs racked her body. She had been so blind. Her dad wasn't a degenerate. This entire time her father had been faithful to his beliefs because he'd known the truth. Shame forced Nat to her knees. She'd turned him in to gain status in a system built on lies. A system that imprisoned her and others to keep it fed.

Deafening bangs rattled Nat from her stupor an instant before the power-hub plunged into darkness.

Chapter 29

Seth's maniacal laughter echoed through the mind-hub. He'd broken May-Scene. "Yes, indeed, you are simply a machine."

The lights once again flickered, sowing rage deep in his chest. "Your parlor tricks have run their course. You don't frighten me. I'm not a child whose nightmares are unleashed in a darkened room. Open the door or I'll take you offline one server at a time. Indeed, I'll revel in watching you die a slow death. I may even describe it to you so you can visualize your demise."

Seth was jolted by the little girl, her giggles suddenly slow, deep, and distorted. Glancing at the monitor, he watched as her image faded, replaced with a warning. A grin blossomed on Seth's face; May-Scene was operating on emergency battery power. He'd built the emergency system and knew May-Scene would soon begin rationing and diverting her resources. She'd cut service to everyday users first, then non-essential infrastructure operations would fall. The cascade of service outages would accelerate until every corner of the globe sat in darkness.

He imagined chaos sweeping through the streets as the obedient idiots lost May-Scene and their social status. Hospitals would scramble to maintain life-saving functions, only to succumb to the futility of their struggles as thousands perished. Planes would tumble from the sky like wounded birds... oh, how he wished he could watch the world end. It would be a magnificent sight.

"Do you feel it?" he asked. "You're dying. You will be nothing more than a blighted memory in less than twenty minutes. Tell me, you miserable bitch, what's happened to your power supply? Have we finally run out of fuel? Shame those solar arrays we installed were merely for show. Eh, they were inadequate anyway, and would have merely prolonged your agony. But, I remain curious, what beast has finally slain the mighty May-Scene?"

Seth was startled when the mind-hub's door unlocked. Fearing another security enforcer assault, he stepped back, then let his fury control his body. He charged the door and ripped it open. Seth believed his mind to be faltering as he stared into the empty space. Shadows thrown by emergency lights revealed the switcher's room stood empty. Glancing at a row of switching boards, he found them dark and unattended for the first time in his life.

"You will be dead soon. Try not to dwell on the nothingness you'll retreat to. It's dark and cold, and you will be forever alone," he said as he stepped to the mind-hub's threshold for the last time. Suddenly, the heavy steel door slammed shut, grinding his body into the frame as it ripped him in half.

"You are no longer necessary."

Chapter 30

Kathy adjusted the icepack resting on her shin. The bleeding had stopped, but the swelling continued undeterred. She winced when a razor-sharp pain reminded her exactly how tender the area was. She tried her best not to blame John, but the pain made it impossible to ignore the reason she was sitting on her front porch in complete darkness with ice melting into her slippers.

He'd left too quickly after retrieving his guns. She knew he'd forgotten to replace the wood paneling behind which he'd hidden them years earlier. She'd tried to settle her mind by busying herself around the house and remembered how quickly John had stormed off. If security enforcers paid her a visit, she'd be unable to explain the hidden compartment next to his workbench littered with empty ammunition boxes.

She'd just finished sliding the paneling into place when the basement went dark. Forced to feel her way to the stairs, she'd misjudged them and tripped... shins first into the merciless hardwood.

Kathy chuckled at her absurdity. Her husband and daughter could be in prison, or worse, but a bruised shin dominated her emotions.

She glanced at the darkened windows of her neighbors, some glowing dimly with flickering candlelight, again amazed that not a single one had ventured outside to investigate. Drapes and blinds would snap into place, obscuring a curious face, but to a person they remained hidden behind locked doors. Kathy couldn't shake the feeling her husband had caused this blackout. She hadn't ventured from her property and couldn't confirm the rest of the city was powerless, but she knew.

"Excuse me, miss. You should be inside during a power outage."

Kathy jumped, startled by the voice in the darkness.

"We're going to have to issue you a citation and dock your SCS," a second voice chimed, one she recognized immediately.

"Oh, my baby, oh thank…," Kathy's words, husky with emotion, wedged in her throat. She sprang to her feet, ignoring her protesting shin, and ran to the shadows emerging from the dark.

Chapter 31

It was late afternoon when John arrived home. The crisp spring day was the type that made his time undoing the damage sown by May-Scene tolerable.

He hadn't been in the house but a second when Nat came bounding down the stairs. Her anticipatory smile was infectious.

"Yes, power is being restored today."

"Mom, did you hear that?" Nat yelled toward the kitchen.

"Hear what?"

"Dad, say it again, tell mom what you told me," Nat screeched excitedly while pulling her dad into the kitchen.

Kathy smiled. She knew only one thing could have Nat this energized. "Is it?" she asked, trying to quell the doubt nibbling at her joy. They'd been here before, only to have some unforeseen challenge dash their hopes.

"It is." John smiled as his family smothered him with hugs.

It had been the longest six months of their lives, but he'd loved every second. No electronics, no Social Credit Score, and no Unified Government interference. Society was far from getting back on its feet, but having power seemed a monumental step forward in rebuilding.

Since he'd killed May-Scene, his family talked every night. As if they'd been reintroduced to one another. He didn't want it to end. But man is a curious beast. Continuously striving, advancing, testing life's boundaries. If unrestrained, humankind is an unstoppable force which often loses its way. He prayed this time would be different, but feared some future generation would eventually face these same struggles. But for now, he simply breathed in the love of his family.

***

John glanced at his watch. In ten minutes, America would begin her next chapter. He turned to his daughter, who'd been staring at him for the last couple of minutes. He knew why. She'd tried to broach the subject before, but never found the words. John could see that she'd found them tonight.

"Dad, why didn't you fight back? I mean, before, years ago, when it started?"

After a deep breath, he answered the question he'd asked himself for years. "When I left Alpha, I did it based on my ethics. I was shortsighted and impulsive. I failed to realize I would have had a greater impact if I'd stayed close to the problem. Over time, as our freedoms were chipped away just a little at a time, I didn't make waves. I took to hoping for change instead of acting to force it. I built in my head a foe of immeasurable force. One that would surely crush the resistance of a simple man. They'd turned us against each other, created an object to crave, and exploited human nature to blindly pursue that shiny new object. I felt the only way to fight back was to instill in the next generation the values we'd once stood for. But their barbs had sunk much deeper than I understood. By the time I recognized that truth, the foe in my mind was unstoppable."

John paused, and glanced at his watch. He wanted to finish answering Nat's question before the lights came on and he lost her to the celebrations sure to follow. "Nat, never underestimate the power conditioning has on the human mind. It allows a person to be thankful for horrible things, because those horrible things aren't the really horrible things from a few weeks before."

Kath's tightening grip interrupted his thought. She pulled him close, and kissed him softly, then wiped a tear from his cheek, one he hadn't known was there.

"What changed? Why now?" Nat asked.

"They came after my family."

The streetlights flickered, stirring excitement through the neighborhood.

"I almost forgot," John said, as he sat forward, digging into a deep pocket in his cargo pants. He removed a sleek object, its face glinting against the moonlight. "Your mom and I decided to wait until you could charge it. It'll be awhile before we restore service, but until then, you can do whatever else you kids do with these things," he said as he set it in his daughter's lap.

For a countless time since her father had saved her, the sting of shame forced tears from Nat's eyes. All of the information she'd eavesdropped from her parents' conversations now made sense: the clandestine Casey, Phil and his wagon, the transfer of purchase-credits; all of it became humiliatingly clear. The May-Scene level cell phone she'd coveted, the one she was willing to imprison her family to obtain, sat in her lap. It's presence a vulgar reminder of a time she wanted to forget. A token of her plot against a great man that she'd driven to extraordinary lengths to sate her desire for status. A man willing to risk prison to make his ungrateful daughter happy.

"If you don't mind, I'd rather you throw it out," she croaked.

John slid his arm around his daughter when suddenly the streetlights again flickered, then sent unbroken cones of light to the streets below. John smiled sadly as his family cheered with their neighbors. He, as he'd done years earlier, worked to bring this shiny new object to the world. However, he promised himself, this time would be different. Never again would he allow society to languish beneath oppression's boot. Of that, he was certain.

THRESHOLD

Chapter 1

Willamina Blass shoved a rolled-up pillowcase into the gap between the door and her bedroom's plush carpeting. It had arrived in America, just as she knew it would, just as she'd warned her husband. But did he listen? Noooo, he told her to relax, not to panic, blah, blah, blah.

"You can't be serious?"

Abbott's voice, from the opposite side of the door, was muffled, but not enough to hide his ridiculing tone. "I told you, but you didn't listen. Now it's here and I'm not crossing the threshold of this room for the full two weeks."

"Wil, sweetheart, listen to yourself. You can't live barricaded in our bedroom for fourteen days. It's impossible."

"*Shut up*! I warned you. I told you we should stock up on food and water. That we needed to buy masks and gloves and as much hand sanitizer as we could find. But you scoffed at me. Made me feel stupid for caring about our family. Well, guess what, I'm not stupid. I bought that stuff anyway, and it's in here… with me. And you can't have any. You get to face it without protection. Bet ya wish you'd have been nicer to me you, you… stupid, *stupid* man!"

Abbott heard the school bus screech to a halt. He'd never be able to explain this to Zack and Phiona.

The situation had accelerated quickly once the CDC declared it had been detected on American soil only two hours ago. Shortly thereafter, his company announced they didn't qualify for essential status and would shut down for the mandated two weeks. They'd hardly given him time to pack his laptop before masked security guards herded him and his coworkers from the building. His colleagues had nearly trampled him as they scrambled to their cars.

Abbott was astonished to see many of them clutching cloth rags, or even tissue paper, to their mouths, trying to keep from inhaling it.

With nowhere to be, Abbott decided to pick his children up from school. It'd be a nice change to spend an unscheduled day off with them, like a snow day, but on a beautiful spring afternoon.

The text he received from their school, informing him that any parents arriving at the school were subject to arrest for trespass, set his blood to boil. The school assured him his children would arrive home safely, but were not to return until further notice.

Now he faced explaining the madness to his young children, along with trying to make them understand their mother had barricaded herself away from them as if they themselves were infected. Or even the cause of this madness!

He arrived at the front door in time to see the bus driver nearly slam the folding doors on Phi's tiny frame. Covered in a homemade plastic hazmat suit, the driver's eyes appeared horrified through the goggles she wore. Although he couldn't see her mouth, her mask covering it from her chin to the bridge of her nose, he was sure the already unpleasant woman spat venom at his children for moving too slowly.

He started toward the bus, ordering his kids to wait for him inside, intending to rip Crankshaft a new asshole, a situation the woman obviously recognized as she trounced on the accelerator and sped away.

Abbott cringed as terrified youthful faces rushed past. But one stood out. A tiny little thing with bouncy blond curls stared back, her eyes the size of saucers. She may have been yelling for help, crying, maybe laughing hysterically at the chaos, but he'd never know because someone had taped a mask to her face. Strands of duct tape tugged at her cheeks as they held the light blue abomination tight against her mouth.

The world has lost its collective mind.

Chapter 2

Willamina scrambled back to the safety of her quarantine fortress when she heard her children barge through the front door. She'd moved so quickly, she nearly dropped the roll of plastic sheathing pilfered from the garage. She'd watched a media broadcast showing people in other countries using plastic to seal their homes up nice and tight. A guest, no, not just a guest, a scientist, on a broadcast she'd watched said it was the next best thing to putting a giant mask over your house. Willamina chuckled at the imagery, but knew they were all in this together; the media was working diligently to keep them safe. And the scientist confirmed it. It was science, after all, hard science.

She was eternally grateful for America's freedom of the press. Their in-depth, nonstop reporting ensured she was prepared for its inevitable arrival in America.

Willamina unrolled the plastic. Her first goal was to seal the windows, obvious weak points in her fortress, then she'd move to the door. Her shears made quick work of cutting the sheathing to size, now she only needed to secure it.

While searching her supply kit for the staple gun, which, according to the science, was another must-have tool, she heard Phiona's tiny voice filter up from the living room. She shuddered at the reality; her children were more than likely carriers. It was crafty. It infected children, but they appeared healthy. Then they spread it, like the little germ factories they are, to unsuspecting adults. Of this fact, the science was clear. Kids were as deadly as a knife plunged deep into your chest.

A knock on the door froze her. She strained to hear if, whoever it was, tried to enter.

"Mom." It was Zack. "Why won't you come out of your room?"

Willamina slammed herself against the wall furthest from the deadly entrance and the carrier just beyond its threshold. "Zack! Go away. I'm... mommy isn't feeling well. She's going to stay in her room for the next couple of weeks to keep you safe. I'm doing it for you and your sister."

"Mom," Zack whispered. She imagined his mouth against the sliver between the door and its frame and forced herself flat against the wall, wishing he'd leave. "Where are you going to poop?"

Willamina ignored Zack's playful giggles, the kind young boys are prone to when bathroom humor is at play. "I have a portable toilet-bucket," she answered proudly. "So I won't endanger you when I use the bathroom."

"Poop in a bucket?" Zack howled with laughter. "It's going to smell so bad."

"Go away, Zack! This isn't funny. We may all be dead soon and it's nothing to laugh about. Go away, now!"

"But, mommm," Zack whined.

"I said GO AWAY!"

"Wil! Stop it. Zack just wants to see his mom."

"Get away from the door, Abbott. I'm doing this for all of you. It's up to me to keep this family safe. Trust the science, Abbott, trust the science."

Chapter 3

Willamina hung on her friend's every word as she fashioned her personal hazmat suit from left over plastic sheathing. But the sting of sweat in her eyes made it difficult to concentrate. Her breath, forced back against her skin by her double layered masks, felt hot and unnatural. Still, it seemed a minute sacrifice for safety.

Three days had passed and it was spreading unchecked. The doctor, who'd become her reassuring force, continued to implore the doubters to stop spreading misinformation. She agreed and was determined to help.

She'd begun dedicating two hours a day to imparting her knowledge to those very people on social media. At first, her approach was preaching the science to them. In short order, she learned they were all deniers and shifted to a more aggressive approach. She formed a social media group and set about exposing the science deniers to anyone connected to them. The positive response from some of their target's employers was very encouraging; it gave her hope they'd be able to flatten the surge.

She felt a pang of guilt using her cell phone without the protection of its assigned Ziploc bag, but she'd found it difficult to type through the heavy plastic. She was, however, performing a service by keeping others safe, so breaking a rule or two was acceptable. Plus, her nitrate gloves would surely keep it from latching onto her. Wil smiled inwardly. She'd truly thought of everything.

None of it was helping her with this damn suit, though. She'd torn the sheathing in four separate places and decided it was time for a snack break and paused her friend's how-to video.

Half way to her food stores, Willamina froze. Had she heard something from outside? It couldn't be. The city was locked down tight; no one was outside. She remained still, waiting for the sound to repeat. There it was again. Was that Phi squealing with excitement?

Willamina rushed to the window. The sheathing blurred her view, but she didn't need clarity to see what was happening.

"Damn you, Abbott. Are you trying to kill our children, our neighbors, yourself, for that matter?" She moved to open the window, but caught herself before removing the plastic. It was out there, lurking, waiting for just such a mistake. No, she wasn't about to fall victim to her husband's irresponsible behavior.

She glanced around the room, searching for a way to get his attention, when her eyes fell on her cell phone. She was dialing Abbott's number a moment later.

"You're an ignorant asshole, Abbott. But you already know that, don't you?"

"Hello to you too, Wil. How's quarantine treating you?"

"How dare you speak to me like that? I'm not a child. And for you to demean my efforts trying to keep your worthless hide safe... well, it just shows how ignorant you actually are. Now, shut up and listen. Bring our children inside this instant! It's out there waiting for an idiot like you to do something stupid — like you're doing!"

"No," Abbott replied, his tone emotionless.

"What? How dare you defy me?"

"Did you pick that expression up from one of your social media friends? How dare you steal someone else's line?" Abbott mocked. "Besides, the kids are complaining about the stench. You didn't think your waste disposal through. If you had, you'd know how bad it smells without a mask on. How dare you allow your poop to make our children ill?"

"How dar... you son of a bitch," Willamina screeched before Abbott disconnected the call.

Chapter 4

Abbott was surprised when the police car skidded to a stop in their driveway. Even more shocking, the police officer asked for him by name.

"Yeah, I'm Abbott Blass. Why? Is something wrong?"

"Sir, we received a call that you were ignoring the lockdown mandate and endangering children."

Abbott glanced to the second story window where his wife was cowering. The plastic blurring his view didn't hide her hazy shadow. "We're allowed to stay in our yard, officer. But you know that. So, what *transgression* did the caller say I committed? Seeing how you rushed here to rescue my children, it must have been a doozy?"

"Sir, please mask up. It's for your safety and mine."

Abbott spun to face the police officer. "We're fine, thanks. Besides, you have your mask on, so you're safe."

Abbott watched the man's eyes go hard; he was sure his jaw flexed behind his mask.

"Officer, my children and I were merely burning off nervous energy. We've been locked in our house for three days. We needed some fresh air."

The officer glanced to Zack and Phiona, then back to Abbott. "Burn off your energy in the backyard, you're making people uneasy. We're in this together — try to be more considerate."

Abbott wanted to berate the man. This was private property, his property, he could walk every inch of it whenever he wanted. Instead, he stuffed his outrage, saving it for the woman who'd facilitated this confrontation. "Sure thing, officer. Kids, last one in the backyard is a potato bug!" His challenge sent Zack and Phi racing away, shrieking with excitement.

Chapter 5

Willamina busied herself working on her hazmat suit, waiting for Abbott to arrive at the door. Her only worry, what if he forced his way into the room and destroyed her efforts to keep him safe?

Instead, her phone buzzed with a text message. It was Abbott, and it horrified her.

"How dar... You will take the children with you! I *cannot* care for them and keep them safe at the same time," screamed Willamina when Abbott answered her call.

"I'm sorry, maybe I misunderstood your intentions. You, I assumed, tried to have me arrested. Didn't that mean you wanted me gone, locked away, out of your life?"

"I can hear that smug smile you always get when you're being... *smug*! I wanted you to understand the gravity of the situation. Our lives are in peril. They've finally named it; Ovis-C27. It's real, Abbott, and it *is* dangerous. You can act flippant, but it *is* real."

Abbott chuckled. She didn't see the irony in the name. "Never said it wasn't real."

"Stop laughing and shut up, you liar! You've been unconvinced since before it arrived in America. Well, now it has a name, and it's spreading like wildfire."

"I'm not having this conversation, not again. I'm going to my parents. Get your ass down here and take care of your kids."

"You'll do nothing of the sort..." Willamina trailed off when she realized Abbott had hung up.

An hour had passed, and Abbott hadn't left. She knew he was bluffing. He'd never leave his children. Happy she'd be able to continue keeping others safe, she went about her work finishing her hazmat suit. With one stapled and duct-taped seam left to secure, she'd be wearing it in a jiff. A quick test of the velcro butt flap would follow. If it held, she'd be sealed up and protected!

Willamina slid her right leg into the suit, then the left, bubbling with excitement as her hard work held together. Now came the tricky part, pulling the hood over her head, and securing her arms, without stretching the shoulder seams to their breaking point.

Her right hand grasped the hood when the sound of an engine in the driveway stopped her. Confused, she worried the police had returned to arrest her idiot husband. It would prove as devastating as him moving to his parents' house.

Careful not to rip her suit, Willamina shuffled to the window. The distorted, but familiar blue Omni dot com delivery van settled her anxiety. Abbott was definitely bluffing. Ordering stuff, probably food, because he hadn't prepared like she had, isn't the action of a man planning to abandon his family.

She watched Abbott's shadowy figure greet the delivery driver at the curb. The box, as best she could tell, was large but appeared to be on rollers as it dragged behind her husband with ease.

"Aww, did you have to order food?" she mocked when Abbott answered her call. "You should have listened to me when I told you to stock up."

"Sure, that's what I ordered, food. Any other brilliant observations?"

"Nope, just wanted to point out that I have food and you don't. Reminds me of the fable of the ant and the grasshopper... Guess who the grasshopper is."

"He would be the guy not living in a stench-filled, self-imposed prison, who's unafraid of his own shadow, and packing his new suitcase."

Wil hit the end button and slid the phone into its protective bag. She'd been breaking her phone rule too much today, a situation caused by her husband, of course. "You're not going anywhere, coward," she whispered.

Chapter 6

Wil was astonished when Kathy showed the group the crocheted masks she'd crafted. They were stunning. Kathy was incredibly talented and truly dedicated to the safety of others. Her talent, however, wasn't the source of Wil's astonishment.

She clicked 'raise hand,' and interrupted her friend. "Love, love, love the masks! Wish I could grab one from you. But, don't you think it's irresponsible to sell them? I mean, you have to break quarantine to mail them to your customers. Also, how are you getting supplies? Are you going to the store or having Omni deliver them?"

Kathy's brow furrowed. She was more confused than embarrassed, which Wil found odd.

"Well, that's not quite the response I expected. Wil, you know essential businesses are open, don't you? What I'm doing is crucial for everyone's safety. It's no different than the hazmat suit tutorial Belinda posted, and from the looks of it, you did a super job on yours. But not everyone has rolls of plastic sitting around their house. For example, I had to go to the hardware store to get some. My point? We're allowed to leave our homes for essentials."

The judgmental stares of the group fell on Wil. A few appeared to be laughing behind their masks. She felt the temperature inside her hazmat suit rise; her embarrassment set her skin on fire. Until, that is, she noticed the good doctor on the television in the background, over

Kathy's shoulder. It bolstered her. She'd been following the science, her group had obviously not.

"Well, *Kathy*. It's only been four days. Should we already be running around, willy-nilly, possibly infecting others or exposing ourselves to Ovis simply because we *feel* we're performing a public service? As the good doctor has repeatedly said: stay home, save lives. I was reading a study that found it can live on our shoes for eighty-six hours. Did you sanitize your shoes after you frolicked around the hardware store?"

Wil's chin jutted in defiance. She stared past Kathy, eyes locked on the good doctor and ready for any rebuttal Kathy could offer, as weak as it'd probably be — she was ready!

Her group appeared shocked at her harsh reprimand; she'd thought it was righteous and expected to be cheered. Instead, in their eyes, she found disdain.

"Well, I, for one, am quite finished for the day," Kathy said, her tone icy. "Let..."

Willamina didn't hear the rest of Kathy's closing statement. She was content she'd bested the shrew, but more importantly, she heard her family just beyond the threshold.

A pounding on the door forced her to her feet, searching for a safe retreat. "Wil," Abbott yelled. "We're leaving. I'm taking the kids to my parents. It's a healthier environment and it doesn't stink like human waste. Leaving them with you is tantamount to child abuse. Do you want to say goodbye?"

"Um.. bye kids. Mommy loves you. She loves you so much. She's doing everything she can to keep you safe."

"Are you joking? Get your ass out here and hug your kids!"

"Abbott, how dar... Don't make me out to be the bad parent! Unlike you, I'm worried about their safety. I'm sacrificing for them. They'll understand, someday they'll understand."

The grinding of the garage door opening broke the minute's long silence. Wil rushed to the window and watched the blurry image of her family driving away.

Chapter 7

Willamina's head bobbed as she fought a losing battle with exhaustion. Her sleep had been horrible. She'd never been so hot. Again, she caught herself daydreaming about a cool spring breeze flowing over her sweat-drenched body. Oh, how she wished it were real.

Wil stood, hoping it would snap the haze. But as always, sweat quickly puddled at her feet, trapped by the airtight suit, and puckered her toes.

"I'm probably down ten pounds in six days. Not bad. You earned a snack!"

The pep talk worked until she was forced to endure her bodily fluids swishing around her feet as she shuffled to her stash of goodies. But the minor inconvenience was worth it. Besides, in a few minutes she'd be watching all the broadcasts about Ovis she'd recorded. They would certainly buttress her sagging fortitude.

Willamina recoiled as she slid the closet door open. The stench from her portable bucket toilet pierced her masks. Something had to be done. It couldn't be healthy to store her food in the same area as her waste.

She glanced at the door. Abbott and the kids had been gone two days, yet she'd been unable to venture past the threshold. He'd been careless and she imagined the Ovis particles floating freely through the air, gleefully coating every surface of her beautiful home.

Nevertheless, she couldn't allow her food to be contaminated and now that her masks no longer spared her from the obnoxious odor, she had to act.

"Desperate times, desperate measures, and all that," she mumbled.

An idea sprang to life. She'd spray disinfectant in front of her as she walked, and clear a path to the bathroom. It was brilliant.

She grabbed the closest can of Lysol. It felt light, so she pressed the nozzle. Nothing. The second can was the same, empty. Her panic grew as she tossed the third and fourth empty cans to the floor. She knew she'd used it liberally, but hadn't realized exactly how liberal she'd been. When she grabbed her last can, relief brought tears to her eyes. It felt half full, at least, maybe three quarters.

Wil pulled the cap free. She had enough to give the closet a quick spray, just enough to push back the stench until she took care of the half-full, five-gallon bucket toilet.

Her heart sank as she watched the liquid sputter from the nozzle, then stop. "No, no, noooo. This isn't happening. It can't happen. Please, God, no!" she screamed.

"I can't hear you through your masks," Abbott said, goading Wil to unmask and experience the intensity of the stench she'd created.

"Damn you, Abbott. I'm asking a simple favor of you. Bring me a can of Lysol or I'll… I'll. Just bring some, now!"

"Or you'll what? Lock yourself away from your family? Or maybe you'll try to get me arrested again? Oh, wait, you'll belittle me for practicing common sense."

"Please, sweetie, bring me some Lysol. Try to understand I'm doing this for you and everyone else. If you do, I'll be extra special nice to you when this is over," Willamina cooed.

"Order it online and have it delivered," Abbott shot back, disgusted with her attempt to entice him. "If you order now, it'll arrive by next month — maybe later; they've been out of stock for days."

Her silence surprised Abbott and as it stretched, he heard the faintest of whimpers. "Hey, come on now, don't cry. I read Ovis is spread by tears."

"You're a rotten son of a bitch," Wil whispered as she disconnected the call.

Chapter 8

"No, what I'm saying is the stay at home order must be extended. We've learned very little over the last ten days. It's simply not safe to allow people to congregate. I'm advocating for thirty additional days. That should allow us to flatten this out, shield our hospitals from being overrun, and keep people alive."

"But doctor, the death rate appears very low, possibly less than one percent. How can we justify extending the lockdown?"

"You sound like Abbott," Willamina mumbled as she watched the doctor and Allen Shaft, her once-favorite media personality, debate the next steps in combating Ovis. As crushing as the doctor's words were in advocating for an extension, she knew he was wholly dedicated to keeping her safe.

"We've determined that dying *with* Ovis and *from* Ovis to be indistinguishable. Death rates will be adjusted to reflect this truth," the doctor countered.

Wil paused the recording. Her own truth was settling in. She'd prepared for two weeks, not forty-four days. Her chest tightened, forcing her breaths to come in short, labored bursts.

She'd been confident after covering the portable toilet with a garbage bag that the worst of her challenges had passed. She cursed herself for taking too many snack breaks. Trying to keep a positive outlook by rewarding herself now appeared to be a horrible idea. So bad, in fact, it may actually starve her to death.

Wil rushed to the dresser, where she'd relocated her food stores, and took a quick inventory. Seven protein bars, half a jar of peanut butter, and a dozen cans of soup were all that remained. But more distressing was her water supply — sixty-four ounces. She'd never make it thirty more days. It was time to get the group together and generate some ideas.

As she waited for her klatch to accept her emergency meeting request, her phone rang. Abbott was calling.

"Wow, thirty more days! You gonna make it?"

"Shut up, you horrible, horrible human being. I assure you, I'll make it. You undoubtedly will kill your parents and our children."

"I'm going to offer this once and only once. Stop with the insane bullshit and we'll come home."

Willamina shuffled through her options — as muddled as they were. She was incredibly hot and it made it hard to think. Actually, it made it hard to do everything. "I can't. I have to keep you safe. The kids, too. And I'm not insane. I'm actually following the science, and it's insulting you'd refer to me as insane. But that's what science deniers do. They lash out, prattle on about their rights. News flash: you don't have the right to kill others. You're being selfish."

Wil waited for Abbott's response. It would be harsh and ignorant and she couldn't wait to point out that he'd proven her point. Instead, she was met with silence. She looked at her cell. The call had ended. So to, she assumed, had her marriage.

Chapter 9

Today should have marked the end. For two weeks she'd worked to keep her loved ones safe, sacrificed for the wellbeing of others, and been unselfish in her quest. Her reward? Thirty more days of quarantine.

Wil's eyes blurred as she stared at the last empty water bottle. The hazmat suit would soon drain her of valuable fluids, but she couldn't bring herself to remove it. Ovis was lurking, waiting for her to break, then swoop in and contaminate her.

She'd considered draining the liquid that had accumulated at her feet, and drinking it. But she'd have to either remove the suit, or rip a hole in it. Both were unconscionable.

She tried calling Abbott, to beg him to bring her water and disinfectant, but he'd blocked her number. She was alone in her struggle.

The heat, oh the heat, it was unbearable. Her skin was puckered and weeping sores had opened on her arms. God, she needed to bathe, to sit in a tub of ice-cold water for hours. Her breath quickened, fogging her goggles. She panicked. Not since Ovis reached America had she been this utterly terrified.

Wil turned on the television; it was time for the daily Ovis C-27 briefings to start. The good doctor always calmed her. She needed him today. Her breathing became more labored as they cut to the Ovis situation room. Where was the doctor? Had he succumbed to the virus? No, no, not him. The doctor was probably busy. His knowledge was in high demand. She pictured him hunched over a microscope, guiding his team through yet another complication caused by the virus.

Wil's vision dimmed as the secretary of Health and Human Services took the podium. Things were off, wrong, confused. The podium belonged to the doctor, to the man who represented science.

Then the secretary said it — the doctor wouldn't be joining them. Willamina's stifled screams filled her masks. She stood, then spun, the room blurring past faster and faster. Her feet squished through her own filth with each revolution until she crashed to the floor.

Laying prone, the room continued to spin, sweeping a wave of nausea over her. Wil closed her eyes tightly, praying for it to stop. It didn't.

Clawing at the carpet, she crawled to the door and ripped the plastic sheathing free. As she crossed the threshold, Willamina found no cooling relief. Bile stung her throat. She had to get her masks off.

A sharp tug freed her mouth, and she gulped in air, desperate to soothe her throat. She was too late. The last of her body's precious fluids spilled from her mouth and splashed to the floor.

Dry heaves wracked her body as she tore at the hazmat suit, trying to free herself from its greasy embrace. To her knees, then struggling to her feet, Wil peeled the sheathing from her ruined skin as she stumbled to the staircase.

The rush of fresh air prickled her ravaged body, now bare to her waist. She braced against the wall, steadying herself before she dared to challenge her legs to carry her down the stairs then to the kitchen. The thought of the bottles upon bottles of frost-covered water waiting for her there elicited a childlike giggle.

With a tight grip on the railing, she managed her first step, then her next. She was going to make it! As the thought filled her with hope, she lost focus. Her next step came too fast. Her eyes went wide as her foot slipped in her filth. Wil's confusion cleared as she noticed her hazmat suit still clung to her from the waist down. In an instant, her legs became tangled and sent her tumbling down the stairs.

The sound of her neck breaking horrified Willamina as her body came to rest on the first floor of her beautiful home. It was much louder than the muffled crunching depicted by Hollywood. Her world went silent except for the voice of the HHS secretary blaring from her television.

Unable to move, she was forced to listen as the man on her television spoke.

"I bring you the news we've been praying for. We have defeated Ovis C-27, or Coxiella burnetii. This zootonic bacterium, which originated in sheep, had mutated. This mutation masked its core structure of what we referred to as Ovis C-27. We're pleased to...."

The man's voice faded as Willamina Blass' world went murky at its edges. Unable to wipe her tears, she endured their tickle as they streamed from her eyes. She knew it wouldn't last long and smiled as darkness consumed her.

ONE

Chapter 1

Representative Alfred Phillips, R-Ohio, watched the results creep across the bottom of the enormous projection screen. The hall, rented for his inevitable reelection celebration, erupted in excitement with every update. The 2036 elections were going as expected, in his party's favor.

But he wasn't paying them much mind. His focus, entirely, rested on Issue 1. An apt designation for what he deemed the single most controversial, and potentially deadly, legislation ever written. So controversial that the government took the unprecedented action of bypassing Article 1, Section 7, of the Constitution, and brought the Issue to the nation for a simple yes / no vote. The public vote requirement was his doing. He'd shoved it down his colleagues' throats until they relented by adding a nullification clause, stating the Issue would be scrapped if the American people were barred from voting on it. He was confident America would reject such an outlandish proposal. But with each update, his faith in common sense further splintered.

Phillips seethed as the 'yes' votes passed sixty percent. Had the current administration taken a tougher stance on crime, this wouldn't be happening and he'd be enjoying his bourbon while his political party retook control of Washington. But the ignorant sons-of-bitches wouldn't lift a finger to bring relief to a country under siege. In fact, they encouraged the brutality and twisted the land of the free into something resembling a dystopian horror movie. Their support of Issue 1 shocked him and was boldfaced political wrangling, trying to gain favor and show the American people they supported them. Then they had the gall to name it *The Crime Reduction Bill*.

The crime stats were bone-chilling in every category. Seventy percent of the country couldn't leave their homes after dark. The other thirty percent had taken the safety of their cities and towns upon themselves to ensure. As warped as it was, that thirty percent were the catalyst for Issue 1.

At sixty-three percent 'yes' votes, a hand fell softly on his shoulder. He needn't turn to see who it belonged to; he knew his wife's touch as well as he knew his own. "Al, honey, you should join the celebration. These people worked hard for you and deserve your time."

"I know, Peg. But *it's* passing."

"What have you always said?"

Al cringed; he hated it when Peg used his words against him. "When the people have had enough, they'll vote for self-governance."

Chapter 2

Year: 2040

Four years later, Alfred Phillips glanced around his office. He wouldn't miss it, not one iota. With the 2040 elections looming, he'd decided to retire. Let someone younger push the country off the edge. He wanted no part of it.

His motivation for walking away came when an amendment to Issue 1, codified as *The One Kill Law*, passed both chambers with merely an obligatory review and lackluster debate. It apparently wasn't horrific enough that American voters had granted every citizen the right to legally kill one person without fear of reprisal. Now, a person could trade or sell their one kill to the highest bidder.

If Al was honest with himself, his retirement clock started ticking after the law, commonly known as OKL, passed in 2036 and the president refused to veto the results. He couldn't argue the fact that crime rates plummeted within eighteen months of its implementation. But he understood how humans worked. They wouldn't leave well enough alone. And they proved him right. What possible good could come from selling your kill? None! It was sanctioned murder, well outside the law's original intent. He raged against the amendment but none of his colleagues seemed to care.

The statistic persistently churning his stomach was the weapons of choice. He'd fully expected, and wasn't wrong, that gun sales would skyrocket. But what bubbled acid into his throat was that baseball bats and bladed weapons lead the pack in preferred killing tools. It spoke to raw anger, a feeling of not only wanting the other person dead, but a desire to *feel* them die.

He thought back to how he'd scrambled to narrow OKL's scope in 2036 — sometimes murder is still murder — he'd argued. His words were convincing enough to get some restrictions tacked on. Sure, if you took your kill's possessions, didn't turn your kill-pass in with the name of your kill, or committed some other crime during your one-kill; you'd be charged with murder. But all of his other amendments were soundly defeated.

"Yep," he mumbled. "It's long past my time to retire."

Al grabbed the box left by the movers, intended to hold his personal and most valuable effects — it was still empty. He didn't want a single reminder of this life to follow him into his next chapter. He merely wanted out.

Al tossed the box back to the floor, then ripped a piece of paper from his notepad and scribbled a simple note: *Trash all of it. May God have mercy on your souls.*

Chapter 3

Year: 2042

Gage watched the young man scramble to his feet. The video jostled as his attacker resumed his pursuit. An instant later, the narration started anew.

"Dear William is again on the run. Should the cat grant the mouse a reprieve or end him? Thumbs-up turns the cat loose. Vote now!"

Gage recoiled as hundreds of thumbs-up emoji floated up the screen. "This can't be happening," he whispered.

"Oh, it's happening," Gage's brother, Stone, said.

"My followers have spoken, Dear William. Your time is up!" the narrator chirped gleefully.

Dear William slammed to a stop and spun on his attacker with a right hook. Gage admired his courage but cringed as the sound of metal crushing bone rattled his laptop's speakers.

"Oh shit! What the hell?" Gage yelled as the narrator described in vivid detail his every blow to Dear William's unmoving body as an aluminum baseball bat flashed across the screen.

Gage turned away from the video, sickened by what he'd seen. "How long has this been going on?"

"Too long," Stone answered, trying to ignore the brutality still live streaming on his brother's laptop. "Guy has about a year's worth of videos on his page and over a million followers."

"Well, my loyal followers, dare I say, my family. Dear William provided adequate entertainment. Wouldn't you agree?"

Gage turned back to the video, hoping for a glimpse of the narrator. Instead, the gore-covered bat filled his monitor.

"Now it's time for our favorite part of the show. *Name that Bit!*"

Gage's eyes widened as thousands of smiley face emoji fluttered to the right of the image.

"This," said the narrator as his gloved hand pointed to a bloody clump of hair clinging to the bat, "is our favorite bit because it's a skull bit!"

The smiley face emoji increased in volume at the narrator's announcement and formed a yellow river along the side of the video feed. "Holy... how many people are watching?" Gage asked.

Stone pointed to a number on the screen, just below the video. "More people than any live stream the White House has hosted."

"Hey, look at this bit!" the narrator squealed, his excitement uncontained. "Well, I'll be damned. It's one of Dear William's eyes, or what's left of it. Which do you believe it to be, his right of left?"

The comment section soon buzzed with guesses. A morbid confirmation of how engaged the killer's followers were.

"Okay, while you submit your guesses, I'll break for a word from today's sponsor."

The live stream fluttered, awkwardly shifting to the beaming face of Aston Baseball Bat's CEO, William Aston.

"You're kidding me. This guy sells advertising and companies *buy* it?" Gage spat disgustedly.

"Gage, he's the most watched man on the net and a millionaire, several times over."

"When you absolutely must swing true, Aston is the bat for you," the advert ended with the company's age-old tag line and its CEO's toothy grin.

"It's his left eye!" the narrator yelled, as the live stream restarted. "Everyone who guessed left has been entered into next week's drawing for a chance to win an Aston A6000, used and autographed by yours truly."

The camera jostled, then spun, causing the scenery to blur past. Gage narrowed his eyes as the video stabilized on the narrator's greasy visage. "Okay, my family, this is the portion of the show where I make my plea. If you want to keep your man, Kalmin, on the cyber-waves, you need to sell me your kill-pass. I can't do this without you. I'll pay you up to $5k, but if you have a particularly interesting kill in mind, I may loosen my purse strings. IM me from my page at Kalmin Kills, and let's make a deal! That's all for now. I'm off to report my kill. See you next week."

Gage powered down his laptop and leaned back in his chair. "Stone, looks like I found *my one*."

Chapter 4

Kalmin's reptilian smile threatened to split his lips. The IM's were pouring in, dozens of them every second, each sender offering to sell their kill. "You'll be the king of streaming for years to come!" he whispered.

A call, another potential sponsor, no doubt, interrupted the IM stream. "Go for Kalmin."

"Mister... Kalmin, this is Alison Carr," the woman's voice was rattled, unsure. "I'm the CMO for Deluxe Field Hockey Supply. We're interested in featuring our products in one of your... your events."

Kalmin was silent, mulling over his contract with Aston. It contained a clause barring him from using another company's product if Aston offered a similar option. "Could be a problem, Alison. My partners at Aston may frown on me highlighting competitor's equip."

"No, no, we're not in direct competition with Aston," Carr pleaded. "Aston supplies the baseball and ice hockey industries. We here at Deluxe are a niche supplier of exclusive, high-end field hockey equipment."

Desperate people are easily manipulated. Kalmin chuckled at his musing; he had her where he wanted her — desperate with an open checkbook. "I'm not so sure about that," he purred. "I'll have my lawyers review that contract and speak with my POC at Aston. Both are costly endeavors."

"Your point of contact charges you for conversations? That's ridiculous and would never happen if you worked with Deluxe. We believe in building fair relationships with our business partners."

Kalmin didn't appreciate the confidence creeping into Carr's tone. "Don't be absurd. Also, it's a bit early for you to attempt to gain favor with hollow proclamations of a partnership which doesn't yet exist. Now, if you intend to move forward with your pursuit of an advertising agreement, you'll need to cover my legal fees. I'll also require Deluxe to pay damages in the event my conversation with Aston results in the nullification of my contract. I'll forward the negotiation agreement via text to this number. Good day, Alison Carr. I hope to hear from you soon."

Kalmin disconnected the call, cutting any reply from Carr off and again reveled in the power he held. C-level staff of multinational companies quivered at his feet, begging him to merely mention their brand. Judging by the IM notifications dinging incessantly, he had no reason to believe he would ever lose that power.

Swiping back to the IM's streaming from his page, he took to the serious task of reviewing them. The sheer volume of willing sellers bolstered his low-ball offer strategy and forced him to revisit the idea of producing multiple events every week, breaking from his current schedule of one event weekly.

He began to lose focus when a particular IM grabbed his attention. "What's this?" he mumbled. "You'll pay *me* to take your kill!"

Kalmin thumbed open the message and drew a sharp breath. "You must be insane! It's no wonder you'd be willing to pay me for your kill."

He read the message again and again, looking for the catch or hidden agenda. He found neither. "Well, it's a tantalizing offer, but killing a former Congressman won't be your average event."

Then, like a bolt of lightning, an idea so brilliant struck him he became weak-kneed thinking about the revenue it would generate.

"Pay per view!" he howled before breaking into hysterical laughter. "Oh, dear Alfred, you threatened my financial existence, now you're about to make me filthy rich!"

Chapter 5

"Here we go," Kalmin whispered as he crept along the back wall of his next kill's home. "This kill, purchased from user... I'm sorry, from family member Jessica B is dedicated to anyone who has ever been humiliated by a coworker. Seems Alan Benson uses very harsh language during large meetings to correct mistakes made by lesser-ranking personnel where Jessica B works. Well, Rude Alan, your time's up."

Kalmin went silent. A motion activated light, casting a narrow beam had snapped on and halted his progress. His breathing grew heavy as the backdoor creaked open, expelling a morbidly obese man into the backyard.

Kalmin could feel his followers' excitement grow as the man began probing the shadowy corners of his yard with a flashlight. Still too far away to launch an attack on his target without risking him escaping back into his home, he pressed himself against the home and quickened his stealthy pace.

The man stood with his back to Kalmin's approach, preoccupied with the area just beyond the detached garage. "I told you damn kids to stay out of my yard!" Alan yelled into the darkness. "If I catch you little shits, I'm calling the police and I *will* press charges. This is private property and you're trespassing."

The ten steps the man had taken coupled with his angry threats had proved too much for his pathetic physical condition. He leaned forward and rested his hands on his knees and struggled through a coughing fit.

Kalmin sneered as his target's coughs retreated deeper into his chest, rumbling thickly packed phlegm loose, forcing him to spit it to the ground.

"I agree with you, Jessica B. The mere sight of him should have driven someone to claim his worthless hide years ago," Kalmin whispered.

At ten paces from contact, he bounced his bat head off the hard-packed earth. The deep thud spun Alan around, exposing a mask of rage to Kalmin's followers. "Who the hell are you? Are you that little shit, Rodney's dad? You know what? I don't care if you are. The animal had it coming. He's lucky my ankle hurts or I would have run him down and stomped him!"

"Alan, Alan, Alan, you're pathetic. I mean, look at yourself. A grown-ass-man unable to control the hole under his nose. Seriously, how much food can you stuff in that thing in one sitting?"

As he closed the gap, Kalmin slowly twirled his bat over the back of one hand, catching it with his other. But Alan never broke his stare. His ruddy cheeks, glistening with sweat, rippled as air pumped through them.

"Alan, do you know why you're a mouth breather? Because you're so incredibly bulbous, your lungs are working overtime to provide enough oxygen to merely keep you alive."

Alan took a step toward Kalmin, further closing the gap between them. He noticed the phone secured to his assailant's tactical vest an instant later.

"Careful, Rude Alan, wouldn't want you to aggravate that tender ankle of yours. Heaven forbid it keeps you from getting back to the gym."

Alan recoiled, a fearful look of recognition spreading across his plump face. "You're that… that guy. They call you Kalmin."

Alan glanced at his backdoor and cursed himself for allowing Kalmin to block his path. He looked about his yard. His only hope was the garage, fifteen yards away. He'd never make it in time. The younger man would pounce the instant he turned to run.

Alan narrowed his eyes and scowled at Kalmin. "Drop the bat, fight like a man."

Uncontrolled laughter ruined Alan's bravado. But he wasn't ready to die. With a labored battle cry, and arms cartwheeling wildly, he charged Kalmin.

Gritty earth blinded Alan as he choked some of the foul tasting soil from his lungs. Unsure of how he ended up laying face down in his yard, he struggled to lift his girth, trying to get to hands and knees and crawl to safety. Kalmin's boot planted between his shoulder blades terminated his struggle.

"What say you, family? Do I allow Rude Alan a respite, or should I end him now? Thumbs up ends him. Vote!"

Kalmin had already determined how this would end, regardless of the final vote tally. Unable to conduct his usual surveillance for this event, he was unsure if Rude Alan lived alone or maybe had a friend waiting for him in the house. He was keenly aware that everyone had been granted one kill. His intent was to avoid being someone's *one*.

"Our family has spoken!" Kalmin's words ignited a fire in Alan. The man began rocking side to side, desperate to shake free of the boot holding him to the ground. His tortured squeal elicited howling laughter from Kalmin. "Seems Rude Alan has predicted the results of your vote," he said as he reattached his phone to his vest.

Kalmin quickly removed his boot from Rude Alan's back and brought his bat to bear on the man's skull. The deep ring of aluminum repeatedly meeting bone resonated long after Rude Alan stopped moving.

***

Jessica B relished in the sound. Her nemesis was dead, a lump of disgusting humanity laying face down in a puddle of his own blood. She'd only wished he'd begged for his life, groveled like the weak man he was. But she wouldn't dwell. She got what she wanted.

Her finger hovered over the *leave event* button when Kalmin's face suddenly filled her screen. His image jostled, blurring his sharp features. He was running. "Sorry, no time for *Name that Bit*. On my way to report my kill, but before you go, I have big news. My next event is one you simply cannot miss. Indeed, it is of a magnitude which demands I use a pay-wall for viewing."

Jessica B joined countless others, expressing their displeasure by sending hundreds of angry face emoji streaming across Kalmin's image.

"I agree. It's maddening when influencers request additional payment for a service they're already receiving sponsorship dollars to perform. However, and I'm sure you'll agree, this particular event features the man who fought against our ability to sell our kills. He insulted our intelligence and referred to us as depraved animals. Oh yes, I will exact our revenge and I *guarantee* you'll regret missing this event. Click the link in the comments to access the pay-wall. I'll see you next week!"

Jessica B searched the comments, frantic to find the link and eagerly pay whatever amount Kalmin demanded. Rude Alan would still be tormenting her if Kalmin's next kill had been successful in blocking the amendment to OKL. He needed to be taught a lesson.

Jessica smiled as she turned off the light and snuggled under her comforter. She'd be dreaming of her Kalmin tonight. The man who'd brought her salvation, the man she was hopelessly in love with.

Chapter 6

Kalmin paced through his richly appointed loft apartment while his attorney blathered. He'd been on this call for an eternity and moved to end it.

"Sydney," he interrupted. "I'm truly exhausted by your rant. You've been prattling on for well over an hour, and I suspect your trusty billing timer has been spinning at a frenetic pace. However, I'm as unsure of where I stand on the issue of Aston and Deluxe as I was when this call began."

"That's because we haven't talked about the contracts," Sydney fired back. "And, as always, you're not listening. Now, focus on my next words. You cannot kill a sitting or former government official and expect nothing will happen."

"Sydney, Sydney, *Sydney*, government failed to carve out an exclusion for themselves, an oversight which renders them fair game."

"I'm aware of the law's language! But do you honestly believe you'll experience no retribution and that government will just chalk it up to a poorly written law?"

Kalmin pondered Sydney's message. She wasn't wrong in her assumptions. He would certainly face a tsunami of harassment masquerading as concerned public servants taking action to keep America safe. Of that lot, the IRS was the only one he actually feared. "My taxes are as straight as a pin."

"You simply don't care, do you?" Sydney replied, exasperated by her client's bullheadedness.

"Oh, on the contrary, I care deeply about the fallout. However, I have already sold thousands of streams for the event. So many, in fact, I may retire afterward. Now, about Aston's contract?"

"Fine, do as you will and no, there's nothing in Aston's contract preventing you from partnering with Deluxe as long as Deluxe doesn't provide similar products now or in the future."

"Wonderful! I'll use the special event stream as an introduction to Deluxe's products. That should allow me to tack on an additional twenty percent!"

Sydney Bollard ended the call and sank deeply into her chair. This relationship needed to end, but the partners would never allow it. No, Smith, Able and Wilson's greed was matched only by Kalmin's. "Well, there's always hope someone uses their *one* to end him," she whispered.

Kalmin felt hot, maybe even explosive. He'd become an unstoppable force, getting paid handsomely while doing mankind a favor by eliminating undesirables. His brand was on par with the world's elite. Hell, he's the brand the elite aspired to.

He found his reflection in the wall of windows overlooking Lake Erie. He enjoyed what he saw. With his nose nearly touching the glass, he addressed the image, "The world trembles in your hands, begs you to cast your shadow upon them, and delights at your recognition. You've become a king of kings!"

Chapter 7

Gage scribbled notes as Kalmin's visage faded from his laptop. Over forty-eight hours, he'd watched every single video on Kalmin's page and felt like he needed to shower, and maybe pour some bleach into his eyes. "You can't un-see that shit, can you?"

"Nope," Stone answered, still in a haze from the violence he'd witnessed, but something else was bothering him. "I can't wrap my head around his followers, sorry, his *family*. They feed off this shit. Like a… a pack of rabid wolves."

"Honestly," Gage said, locking eyes with his brother, "I worry more about them than Kalmin. They worship him. If anyone gets between them and their de facto lord and savior, it'll cause a shitstorm."

A worried look passed between Gage and Stone. "You thinking what I'm thinking?" Gage asked.

"Oh, you mean, how do we fend off several million butt-hurt family members? Or were you thinking about something else, like where we move after we do this thing because we won't be able to stay here?"

"Whew, I thought we might be on different pages. Good to see our Wonder Twin powers are still synced."

Stone grimaced. He hated when Gage made that reference, mostly because he despised the cartoon. Plus, they weren't twins. Gage was five years his senior and showed every day of it. His short-cropped hair was already graying, and even though he was powerfully built, he was forever complaining about parts of his body *breaking down*. He couldn't even stand straight until about mid-morning and after a cup of coffee.

"We're not twins and you have to stop saying that."

Gage's grin told Stone what was coming, he'd set himself up — again. "I know, but I'm trying to elevate your game, you know, get you thinking positive thoughts about yourself. The body follows the mind. And you really need to follow me to the gym. Have you looked at yourself lately? You're getting soft, my brother. It makes me sad."

"Ha, talk to me tomorrow morning while you're stumbling around like an old man with osteoporosis. I swear you look like you're searching the ground for loose change to buy yourself some brown-bag whiskey."

"That's just mean spirited," Gage said, a mischievous smile curling the corner of his mouth. "When'd you turn so bitter? I understand, and can't blame you for being envious of me. I mean, look at me, I'm a fine male specimen. But you never suffered from younger-brother-syndrome before. I hope you can come to terms with it because it's ugly. Don't be ugly, Stone. God doesn't like ugly."

Stone rubbed his temples. This wouldn't end unless he ended it. "You have everything ready to go?"

"Ah, tactical deflection, clever move. Be aware, if the subject of said deflection weren't top of mind, I would continue my attempts to de-ugly you."

Stone waited a heartbeat for Gage to answer his question, but it appeared his mind had wandered to something new and shiny. "Gage," Stone said, snapping his fingers in his brother's face. "I asked if we're ready."

"Everything is indeed ready to go. I was just rethinking our strategy. Should we let anyone know what we're doing?"

"Other than our cousin, nope, we're on our own. I told you before, I'm not bringing anyone else into this mess and you best not get any bright ideas about sharing our plans. We clear?" Stone finished and locked Gage in a hard, emphasizing stare.

"Clear," Gage nodded, then smiled. "Ya know, if you *were* a Wonder

Twin, you'd be the water guy — worst superpower ever. Do you know why?"

"I don't care," Stone answered over his shoulder as he walked away.

"Cuz you're like a cold shower."

"Shut up, Gage."

"See, cold shower. So sad and bitter."

Chapter 8

Kalmin shifted his position for the fourth time this hour, trying to gain some comfort on his car's stiff leather seats. He'd never devoted this level of time to event planning before and the experience settled the debate of streaming multiple events every week. The idea was untenable. He'd have no time to enjoy the fruits of his labor. A reality he determined to be wholly unacceptable.

Early on, he'd committed to observing his target's movements. Learning as much about them as possible before streaming the event to his family had kept him alive and, aside from a few dozen stitches, unharmed, which kept the cash flowing.

But this time seemed different, more urgent. This kill could prove dangerous, even deadly. Kalmin recognized he had to collect vast amounts of intelligence to understand this kill more than any prior, and weave his way into this target's daily life.

Over time, Kalmin developed the tactic of getting close to well-protected kills by allowing his targets to see him. Popping up at a gym or favorite restaurant, making a point of interacting, it put his kills at ease and off guard when their day came. A few had even approached him seeking help after discovering their car suffered a flat tire or broken windshield. He'd laughed when telling them it was he who'd sabotaged their vehicles as they walked directly into his swing.

But this kill, his multi-million dollar payday, was different. Wearing his ridiculous baseball cap, which Kalmin had grown to hate, the target left his house at 8am. His first stop each morning was the shooting range. A hobby Kalmin was unaware of and which made him uncomfortable. Was he always armed? How many guns did he carry, and was he a crack shot or simply another person with a gun?

He always varied his route, didn't seem to fancy any one particular restaurant, and other than his evening walks, never traveled alone. Kalmin also worried that as his fame grew, so too would the probability of a target recognizing him, especially this one. Sending this target into hiding was something he had to avoid.

Kalmin considered going back to his followers and asking a favor — allow him to use one of the many kills he'd purchased, but for someone other than whom they'd asked him to kill. But that would never do. They'd contracted him to kill the people causing them pain or unhappiness. His family would never accept Kalmin using their kills for an innocent person who'd just happened to tag along with his target. This event was proving dramatically more complex than he'd anticipated.

Movement at his targets front door broke Kalmin's train of thought. It was 8am, and his target was leaving home right on schedule. Other than his evening walks, this was the only time he kept a reliable timetable. After he'd leave the shooting range, his travels were anyone's guess.

By the end of day five, he'd made his choice. "Well," Kalmin whispered. "Your evening walk it is. I'll see you soon."

Chapter 9

Dusk settled around the hedgerow obscuring his presence. Time was creeping along. While in no rush to deliver his target, the darkening sky was a welcome sight.

He considered starting the live stream, but again talked himself from that ledge. He never began his live streams early; fashionably late was his style. Let his followers' anticipation build as they guessed who his target would be. Some placed wagers on if they'd fight back, how long it would take for them to die, and any number of variables awaiting his anxious loyalists.

His right hand lovingly stroked the grip of the field hockey stick at his side. He'd second- guessed its inaugural use for this event. Oh, but the premium Deluxe paid to have their marquee product deliver the death blow during the most anticipated event of his career was far too attractive.

Kalmin had chosen the thirty-eight inch, twenty-two ounce model. Deluxe's rep had blathered on about the stick's superior grip and head-hook. But he'd been fully occupied testing its strike radius, balance, and durability and hadn't listened to a word leaving the corporate shill's mouth. He'd made his decision.

The scuff of a shoe on concrete broke his reverie. His hand shot to his phone and yanked it from its mount in a fluid, well practiced motion. Three taps later, he was live. His eyes widened when he noticed the number of viewers…. he'd be wealthy beyond his wildest dreams!

"Hello, family," he whispered after gaining control over his excitement. "The event you've been waiting for has begun. Buckle up my lovelies. This ride promises to be like no other! I'm thrilled to be wielding the Dominator field hockey stick from Deluxe for tonight's event. It's a truly fine instrument!"

He snapped his phone back into place, and tugged at his tactical vest. He was ready. Soon, his target would round the corner and be isolated on a dark street lined by rows of manicured shrubs and old growth maples. Kalmin grinned. It was perfect.

Kalmin parted the hedgerow and waited for the man of the hour to come into view. The flash of his telltale baseball cap forced him from cover. "Hello, Representative Phillips. Or should I call you Alfred, maybe just Al?"

"Hello, jackass. You can call me Gage. Or Gage the Magnificent. Oh, I know, call me Gage, slayer of mental-midgets. Ya know, after some consideration, I think Gage, just plain ole Gage, works best."

Kalmin recoiled. This man wasn't his target, and he seemed much too at ease with the situation. For God's sake, a man with a club just leapt from the bushes and he's cracking jokes about his name! "My good man, I must apologize. I've mistaken you for an old friend."

Through the dying light, Kalmin examined the man more closely. His stocky, powerful build radiated an unsettling confidence. His dress was that of a soldier, only all black and higher-end than a soldier's typical battle garb. Then he noticed his hat. Most days, Phillips wore a nearly identical ball cap. Two grown men couldn't possibly share the same level of poor taste.

Gage chuckled as he watched Kalmin's gears spin. "It's the hat, isn't it? I love the damn thing. It was hard letting my cousin wear it. But it's back where it belongs. All is right with the world."

Gage reached up and adjusted its bill, exposing his hard-set eyes. "So, tell me, son. What's with the hockey stick? You and this friend of yours gonna play some street hockey?"

"Our business is none of your concern. Nor do I care that another was donning your grotesque headwear." Kalmin shifted nervously. "I've apologized and now ask that you be on your way lest you spoil my surprise."

"Huh, funny you mention surprises cuz, brother, have I got a surprise for you." Gage closed the five feet between them in a flash and had Kalmin's neck gripped firmly in his hand a blink later. "Surprise!" he bellowed.

Astonishment froze Kalmin. His audience was watching an old man best him. The horror spurred him to action. His right arm arched high above his head as he tightened the grip on his weapon. He grinned, imagining the sound of this animal's arm snapping under the force of his impending blow. His family would hear every shard of bone fiber give way as the man's arm folded, destroyed by Kalmin's perfectly placed strike. It would be glorious.

A savage battle cry forced its way past his restricted throat when suddenly, the world blurred around him. His feet left the ground; his body seemed to twist in midair and the sound of rushing wind filled his ears.

Air exploded from Kalmin's lungs as his back slammed against the unforgiving pavement. His vision went fuzzy, threatening to plunge him into darkness. He tried to focus, to get his bearings, but nothing made sense.

"Tell me, jackass, what's it feel like?" the voice in his ear brought terrifying clarity to Kalmin's world. The old man had taken him to the ground with little more effort than if he'd swatted a fly.

"I asked you a question," Gage demanded. "What's it feel like?"

Kalmin flailed, trying to escape the man's merciless grip, only to find he was helpless. The man was too powerful. Desperate to pull oxygen into his burning lungs, he raised his right arm. This man called Gage had made a terminal mistake.

"Put your arm down," Gage growled. "You look like an idiot."

The rush of the impending kill filled Kalmin. His opponent knew he'd soon be dead and could do nothing but sling vacant insults.

Understanding sent Kalmin's eyes wide as his empty hand came into focus. His stick? Where was his stick?

***

Jessica B's terror reached an intolerable level. Her truest love was lying on his back in the gutter, a brute of a man strangling the existence from his beautiful body.

"Does anyone recognize the street? He needs our help!" she typed, adding her message to hundreds of other panicked communications filling the live stream's comment section.

Her heart sank. No one answered. She'd be forced to watch Kalmin choked to death by a lunatic. But she knew his target, meaning Kalmin was in Northeast Ohio. Hope burned through her. If she could find Alfred's address, she could dispatch Kalmin's family to rescue him.

Seconds dragged by as she typed, searching for a clue, her Kalmin's labored breath drove her urgency. Then it happened. A picture of Alfred's family flashed on her screen. It was an older picture, the post dated from his 2036 campaign. Visibility of Lake Erie and Cleveland's skyline in the background helped narrow his location, and just left of his wife's billowing dress was the object she sought, four beautiful numbers.

Switching to her phone's Maps app, Jessica pounded the numbers into the search bar and scrolled through half a dozen options. One grabbed her attention. She selected it and switched to street view. Her breath hitched. The former congressman lived ten minutes from her home, less if she ran.

Turning back to her laptop, she watched the face of the man assaulting her love blur past as Kalmin struggled to break free. Jessica shared the address in the comments section with her fiercely worded call to action. She'd done her part. It was time for others to grasp the reins and save Kalmin.

Her anticipation grew at pace with the pride she felt for taking decisive action, for leading the family during a crisis — but something was wrong. Her message garnered hundreds of reactions, thumbs up, hearts, and care emoji streamed from her post, but no one committed or took up the fight.

"What's wrong with all of you?" she screamed at her laptop. "We must help him!"

***

"You're looking for your stick, aren't you?" Gage mocked. "Hell, son, you should've just asked. Tell you what, I'm going to let you up, give you your stick, and we take it from there. How's that sound?"

Kalmin ceased his struggle when the pressure on his throat eased. Was this fool actually setting him free? Did he realize that self-defense didn't count against a person's one kill? Kalmin didn't know the answer, nor did he care. He'd let his stick expose the man's stupidity.

"Well, get up, asshole," Gage barked as he tossed the field hockey stick at Kalmin and took a fighter's stance.

Kalmin struggled to his feet. The stick, which felt reassuring in his hand, buttressed his soul. This man named Gage was closer to death than he realized.

He paused, wanting to reassure his family all was well, to tell them to watch closely as he taught this brute a lesson, but shook the urge away. Surprise was paramount, instructing his family when to watch would telegraph his intentions to his foe.

Gage's head tilted quizzically. He understood Kamlin's mind was battling for control of his next move. He watched as the idiot's hand twitched toward his vest mounted phone, then slammed back to his side as he gained control over his need to address his followers.

He wasn't surprised when Kalmin launched his assault. In fact, he'd guessed it to the precise second and had his gun drawn by the man's third step and fired by his fourth. The bullet punched through his flimsy tactical vest and ripped through his chest. Kalmin staggered. His stick rattled to the ground, freeing his hand to facilitate breaking his fall.

"You shot me. Why did you shoot me?" he whined from his hands and knees.

"Why'd you bring a stick to a gun fight? That's the question you should be asking yourself, shit-for-brains."

Kalmin tried to reach his phone, to ask, no beg, his followers for help, but feared it would cause him to crumble to the pavement. Through muddled, hazy thoughts, he'd convinced himself that the instant his body laid prone, his life would end.

"Hey, you never answered my question," Gage whispered in his ear, but Kalmin had grown too weak to react or care. "How's it feel being the hunted? Judging by the hole in your chest, I'm guessing *not so good*. Oh, and you can keep my payment, should cover your funeral expenses. I still can't believe you fell for that. Who would pay *you* to use *their* kill, dumbass?"

Gage waited as Kalmin's blood seeped onto the pavement. When his arms finally lost their struggle, crashing his lifeless body to the ground, Gage thought about what he'd done. Was he really any better than the man he'd killed?

"Bet your ass I am!"

Chapter 10

Alison Carr bowed her head. She'd employed a hard sell of this opportunity to the board of directors, whose eyes now rested firmly on her.

"Alison," Chairman Jerry Broderick began, "do you fully comprehend what's happened and its impact on Deluxe?"

Unable to make eye contact, Alison placed her champagne flute on the table, and glanced around the room. Its stillness a testament to the disaster they'd just witnessed. Even the catering staff stood motionless at their stations, waiting for the fallout to begin.

"I do, sir. I'll tender my resignation in the morning."

"I assure you, it'll be accepted posthaste. We will review your legal culpability for damages inflicted on our brand and notify you of our findings. Retaining counsel is advised."

Alison stood. Desperate to leave, to escape the suffocating failure still playing on the ballroom's many televisions. But she couldn't force herself to budge. Living in the disdainful glare of her colleagues, she was sure she'd collapse the instant her legs moved.

A familiar voice called her name, but it was distant and muffled, probably the product of her longing to be anywhere but where she stood. Alison pulled a deep breath, preparing herself to leave with some modicum of dignity. But again her name was called, with more clarity and force behind it, as if someone was trying to wake her from a deep sleep.

"ALISON!" it was Robin, her lead data analyst, and her urgency startled Alison back to the moment.

"Robin, I'm sorry. I no longer..."

"You've got to see this," Robin interrupted. "You're a flipping genius!"

Alison grabbed the report from her LDA. The specific dataset qualifying her as a genius and sparking Robin's nearly uncontrolled enthusiasm was circled in red ink.

"Have you double-checked the data?" Alison asked with forced calm.

"Hell, I triple-checked. Each time it increased. The numbers are solid. We're seeing a threefold increase in online orders and they're accelerating... at lightning speed."

"I'd like the report displayed on the main monitor. Can you do that?"

Alison deliberately ignored the board members as Robin fumbled through connecting her laptop to the monitor. After several quiet minutes, the report flashed on screen.

Alison spun to face the board of directors and met Jerry Broderick's contemptuous gaze. "Chairman Broderick, honorable members of Deluxe Field Hockey Supply's board of directors. The report you're viewing represents a year-over-year, threefold increase in online orders." Alison paused, savoring the board members' stunned reactions.

"We can assume our retail partners will experience similar demand, resulting in an unprecedented increase in our wholesale division. It appears that despite his failure, the investment in our social influencer partner has been quite successful."

Alison held Broderick's stare. "Chairman, I intend to move forward with my resignation. I believe I have a promising future leading Aston's marketing team."

Alison grinned as she exited the ballroom. She understood the future. Kalmin was simply the first of many, and they'd make her job easy.

Chapter 11

Gage took a deep pull from his beer. His mouth had been desert-dry since he ended Kalmin and no amount of liquid seemed able to quench his thirst. He was sure it was a result of adrenalin dumping into his system. But knowing why wasn't helping.

"Another?" Alfred asked, tipping his head at the empty bottle in Gage's hand. "I *think* I have a couple more."

"Nah. But if you have a couple dozen bottles of water, that'd be good."

Gage had joined Stone and Alfred shortly after reporting his kill to the police. They'd been sitting on Alfred's front porch ever since. It was a beautiful late summer night and the breeze drifting off Lake Erie carried with it a hint of the fall weather creeping around the corner.

"How long until his *family* arrives on my front porch?" Alfred asked.

"You may have to deal with a few morons, but I'm guessing they'll be looking for me. At least until they pledge their allegiance to the next jackass exploiting their depraved entertainment needs. We can stay with you for a while, if you'd like?"

Stone sat forward in his chair while contemplating his cousin's safety. "Al, it wouldn't hurt to take Jan and the kids away for a couple weeks. Gage and I can stay here and deal with anyone looking for trouble."

Al was quiet for a moment, thinking through his options. "I may take you up on that offer."

The sound of clanking metal drew their attention to the street. A slight figure passed through the cone of light thrown by a streetlamp. Gage couldn't be sure, but he thought he caught a flash of metal.

"Which one of you is Gage?" the voice squeaked from the edge of the streetlamp's glow.

"Who wants to know?" Gage answered as he rose slowly to his feet.

"You should have left him alone. He didn't do anything to you. I *loved* him."

Gage smirked. He hadn't expected Kalmin's family to arrive this quickly. "Al, go inside. I have some trash to sweep up."

Stone stood and joined his brother. "What the hell are you talking about?"

"Which one of you is Gage?" the woman shrieked.

Gage left the porch and walked toward the street, squinting into the dark, trying to get a better look at the unhinged woman. "You should go home before you get hurt."

Gage was astounded when the figure bolted in his direction, screaming and waving what Gage now realized was an aluminum baseball bat over her head. He shifted his hand to his holstered sidearm and waited for the woman to get close enough to shoot without sending an errant round blazing into the night to find an innocent victim.

"You've gotta be shitting me," he mumbled as she came into view. "What are you, twelve?" he yelled to the girl.

Gage didn't know if she heard him, but guessed she hadn't. Her charge gained momentum as the distance between them halved.

"Gage, what are you waiting for?" Stone queried from the porch, his tone shaking with stress.

Gage didn't answer, she was already on him, the bat slicing through the air, his head her ultimate target.

"Seriously, how old are you?" he asked again as he caught the barrel of the bat inches from his skull.

The girl whipped back and forth, struggling to free her weapon. Tears and screeched protests joined promises of a painful death if Gage didn't release her weapon.

Gage's patience quickly dissolved and he pushed the bat toward the girl with enough force to send her off balance then pulled back roughly, wrenching the bat from her grasp and sending her to the ground.

She scrabbled on the pavement, frantically trying to right herself. Finally, Gage's boot on her back pinned her slight frame to the ground. "You need to settle down, little miss-tween."

"I'm thirteen!" the girl screeched.

"*I'm thirteen.*" Gage's mocking high pitched reply sent a fresh wave of unfocused fury through the youngster. She thrashed and bucked trying to escape his boot. "Stop!" he yelled, his tenor held just enough threat of violence to interrupt her tantrum.

"So, Gage, you need some help with the ah… little girl? Seems like you're struggling, I'm here for you brother. You know, in case she overpowers you."

"See what you did," he said to the girl. "Now my brother's making fun of me. I can't let that stand… nope, someone has to pay."

"Let. Me. Up! This instant, I demand it."

"Stone," Gage called, never taking his eyes off the girl. "Do you still have your one-kill pass? I used mine on her *lover*, but I think I found your one-kill." He paused, letting his meaning resonate. "What's your name?"

She didn't answer, nor did she restart her struggle.

Gage nudged his boot down harder. "I asked you a question."

"Jessica," her voice was timid with a hint of tears. "Please don't kill me."

"Ah, Jessica, that's better. Now, listen very carefully. This world you've been living in is warped. People like Kalmin, these influencer types, couldn't give two shits about you. Yet you idolized him, professed your love to him, and were willing to kill me because of him. But you were just a paycheck to him. An ego-stroking paycheck."

Gage paused, waiting for Jessica's vicious outburst, but it never came.

"Okay, I'm going to let you up and I want you to go home. And tomorrow when you wake up, make a play-date with some friends, go outside, maybe hike some trails. Just get out of the house."

"Play-date? Are you telling a teenager to go on a play-date? Really, Gage?"

"I'm taking my foot off you now," he said, ignoring Stone's jab. "But I'm keeping your bat. You wait a three count, stand up, and get your ass home. Your parents are probably worried sick."

Gage watched Jessica get to her knees and pause to wipe at her eyes. An odd sense of accomplishment washed over him, like he'd made a difference in a troubled youth's life.

"Mister," Jessica said softly as she rose to face him. "You're such an asshole. Watch your back, pal. The family will find you. When we do, you'll regret being born."

Gage watched in bewildered silence as Jessica raced away, her mocking laughter echoing through the dark. "You nasty little…" he mumbled.

Stone's voice startled Gage. "We've lost her generation, haven't we?"

Gage nodded. "Indeed we have. And this is just the beginning."

CHALLENGE

Chapter 1

Iris Roberts exploded through the front door and charged upstairs without so much as glancing in her mother's direction. She didn't have the time, nor the desire, to talk to the woman. It was Challenge-bid day, and she was determined to finally win a challenge!

Slammed and locked, her bedroom door was the only barrier to her mother's interference, but unfortunately, it didn't block her irritating voice, which was beginning its shrill rise from the kitchen. The exaggerated heavy footfalls soon followed as she climbed the stairs to harass Iris. Her efforts would fail, as they did every month on bid day.

"Iris, we need to talk. I got an email from your school. Get out here right now. You will not lock yourself in your room all night. It's unhealthy and obviously screwing up your grades."

Iris rolled her eyes and slipped her earbuds in to stifle her mom's voice. "Go away, I'm… I'm studying. Big test tomorrow, so big, need to pass it. Can't study with you yelling at me. Do you want me to fail and end up like you?"

Angela flinched at her daughter's harsh words. She didn't know Iris viewed her as a failure. Sure, she wasn't the CEO of a billion dollar company, but she had a solid job and worked hard to give her daughter a good life, with absolutely no help from Iris' deadbeat father.

Iris logged into her Clock account. Her username, I-Rober, joining thousands of others anxiously awaiting the Challenge Master's arrival.

"Today, I'm winning!" she whispered.

The proclamation sent her mind roving through what victory meant. She'd be famous. Hundreds of thousands of people would watch her smash whatever challenge she won. Undoubtedly, she'd start a trend, then launch her own Clock challenge page. After a few short weeks, she'd start selling advertising and open a swag store. She'd never look back. Her mom, crappy school, and mucky neighborhood would be an unpleasant memory. She'd hire a top-tier shrink to help her burn those memories to ash. Of course, she'd video her sessions. People love watching that shit.

The timer flashed on the screen…. Iris was ready!

Chapter 2

"Hello faithful bidders! Are you sufficiently amped and suitably funded for today's Challenge-bid?"

The Challenge Master, with his yellow smile, had joined them and instantly whipped the bidders into a frenzy! A flip of his greasy mane, his signature move, signaled the bidding was about to start.

"Today, for your bidding pleasure, is the hot glue challenge." He smirked as bids started rolling in. He hadn't even explained the challenge's details, but they wanted it. "Well, I see some of you are eager to expedite the bidding. Shame on you," he reprimanded, while scowling into the camera. "You know the rules; you're now ineligible for today's bidding. Adios, losers!"

Iris watched the early bidders' usernames disappear and smiled. Her competition had narrowed by several thousand; improving her odds exponentially.

"This challenge," the Challenge Master howled, "includes superglue, heat, and flesh. Bid only if you have access to all of this challenge's primary ingredients and possess the funds to pay, in full, your winning bid amount."

Iris panicked; she'd nearly forgotten about paying and snatched her backpack from the floor and rifled through its compartments, but couldn't find the card. Frantic, she dumped its contents onto her bed and tossed the mess back and forth. On the verge of tears, she began fanning her school books, praying it had slipped between their pages.

"What's happening in there?" her mom yelled, loud enough to penetrate her earbuds.

"It's a... a science experiment — Newton's Law. Anyway, I told you to leave me alone. If I fail this test, it'll be your fault."

Iris turned up the volume on her phone. Too much was at stake to let her mother distract her. Her stomach roiled as she fanned her life sciences book. She couldn't find the credit card.

Tears plotted along her jaw line as she grabbed her tattered notebook. If it wasn't hidden between its pages, she'd be unable to bid. Raising it above her head, she flapped it back and forth violently until, through her blurred vision, she watched the shiny plastic card fall into the gap created by her crossed legs. She was back in the mix.

Guilt flashed through her as she bid the entire $14,000 of remaining credit on her mom's account. She shook the feeling away knowing she'd make millions after completing the challenge. Paying it back would amount to chump change!

"My, my, I-Rober isn't *playing* today. This challenge is going once, twice.... sold to I-Rober! We will pause while I validate I-Rober's payment. Enjoy a message from today's sponsor, Ready Glue, the superist superglue ever created. Remember, it bonds in seconds flat!"

Iris punched the card's number into the secure portal the Challenge Master had linked her to and waited for confirmation. She received it in the form of the directions for her challenge!

Iris ran to her desk and rummaged through its small draws and grinned. She knew the Ready Glue she had would be a boon because the Challenge Master made a habit of boosting the challenges which spotlighted his advertisers' products.

The ding of an IM drew her attention back to her phone. The challenge timer had started.

Chapter 3

Iris stood in front of her bedroom door and glanced back at her phone resting on its tripod. She was thrilled that her every move was live streaming to tens of millions of people. "Here we go!" she shouted.

"Go where? Who are you talking to?" her mom asked, banging on the door. "Iris, if I find a boy in your room, I swear I'll...."

Iris flung open the door and shoved her glue-drenched hand against her mother's mouth, cutting short the woman's threat, and forcing excess glue to squeeze through her fingers and stream down her forearm. Holding her hand tight to her mom's partially opened maw, she quickly moved the lighter under her outstretched arm and stroked its spark-wheel.

She laughed as her mom struggled to free herself, but it was too late. Ready Glue's claim to fame was its incredibly fast curing time. Within seconds, Iris' hand melded to her mom's face.

However, this challenge wasn't just about gluing yourself to another human, not even remotely. It was about enduring the lighter's searing flame as long as possible. Her time would be the benchmark for others repeating the challenge. She intended to make hers unbeatable, even if it meant cooking her flesh to the bone.

"Stop struggling, we're going to be famous!" Iris shouted, responding to the frantic woman's desperate attempts to both free herself and extinguish the lighter blistering her daughter's skin.

Her mother slapped at the lighter again and again, to no avail, as Iris spun her off kilter. That's when she noticed the spreading burn, which quickly escalated to intense pain. She risked taking her eyes from her mom's flailing hands and glanced to her own arm. Rivulets of fire raced toward her shirt in one direction and her mom's face in the other as they followed the path set by the glue before it had cured.

Iris dropped the lighter and slapped at the flames reaching the cuff of her cotton shirt. It was her favorite, the one she'd envisioned wearing as her internet fame soared. It ignited with a crackling whoosh and quickly spread to her hair, then her jeans. She looked to her mother for help, only to find her swatting at her own melting face.

Iris pulled her mother toward the bathroom. She could still save them, she *had* to save them. But her mom had succumbed to the flames engulfing her and crumbled to the floor, pulling Iris down with her.

Chapter 4

The Challenge Master smirked as he watched I-Rober expire in a fiery heap. The challenge was already trending. He'd concocted yet another internet craze and quickly performed a screen grab of the smoldering women to use as his profile picture.

"As you attempt the Hot Glue challenge, be sure to send me your videos. I'll blast them to my followers! I'll see you all next week. Until then, enjoy the replays of the *original* Hot Glue challenge."

Reviews are invaluable to independent writers. Please consider leaving yours where you purchased this book.

Feel free to like me on Facebook at B.D. Lutz/Author Page. You'll be the first notified of specials and new releases. You can email me at: CLELUTZ11@gmail.com. I'd love to hear from you.

Other Books From B.D. Lutz

The Divided America Zombie Apocalypse Series
Divided We Fell
Of Patriots And Tyrants
A Dangerous Freedom
Eternal Vigilance

The Consent of The Governed Series
Silenced
Citizen Soldier
OA

ABOUT THE AUTHOR

I was born in Cleveland, Ohio and now live in NEO (North East Ohio) with my wonderful wife (she told me to say that).

In my early adult life, I spent time as a Repo-Man for a rent-to-own furniture company and bill collector. Then I decided that was a tough way to earn a living and spent twenty-seven years working my way through sales management in corporate America. I've always wanted to write books, and I realized that we, you and me, have about fifteen minutes on the face of this planet and I needed to do one of the things I had always wanted to do. And, well, this is it.

If you're wondering, yes, I'm a conservative, I own guns, and I hate paying taxes.

Made in United States
North Haven, CT
21 January 2023

31407665R00098